MURDER BY THE SEA

A tale of murder, intrigue, love and justice
in the reign of good Queen Anne

Martin Craven

A drawing of St. Peter's Church, Owthorne, taken from George Poulson's *History of Holderness*.
The chancel of the church was unroofed in 1793. 'The whole Church was unroofed (sic) and part lead to Rimswell toward a new church and on February 16 1816 the Tower fell with a tremendous crash and on October 11 1824 the last vestage went down being a part of the South wall.' (Document in the author's collection.)

Published by:

Martin Craven
43 Davenport Avenue
Hessle
HU13 0RN

Copyright © 2009 Martin Craven
ISBN 978-0-9564072-0-7

Printed by Kall Kwik, Hull

Chapter One

It was the year of our Lord 1708, in the reign of good Queen Anne. At the Holderness village of Owthorne by the German Ocean nothing seemed to be out of the ordinary. There, and from time immemorial, men when hardly more than boys would earn their bread in the fields, marry in the parish church and live out their lives in the village; women, when hardly more than girls would do likewise, marrying in the church and raise their children. Most would become widows, and at the end of their days would be buried beside their husbands in the churchyard.

The village itself could lay no great claim to fame other than a certain antiquity. Mentioned in Domesday, it had become a part of the domain of the earls of Albemarle, lords of the Seigniory of Holderness under the Crown.

Tradition related that in ancient times two sisters, both wealthy landowners, decided to build a church at Owthorne. Unfortunately, soon after they had agreed on this holy plan, temporal difficulties beset the enterprise. The sisters could not agree on the design for their church, and the quarrel that ensued could only be resolved by the sisters going their separate ways; one to build a church at Owthorne, the other determined to raise her own church at Withernsea. Tradition could not name the sisters, nor even when the event took place, but from that time on the two churches became known as 'the Sister Churches'.

Whilst the parish area was extensive and included the hamlets of Waxholme, Rimswell and South Frodingham, Owthorne consisted only of two large, open arable fields farmed in the time-honoured fashion of alternate crops and fallow. In the summer of 1708, the Northfield was a patchwork of wheat, barley and beans, whilst it was the turn of the Southfield to remain fallow. The men of Owthorne farmed their strips of land, randomly situated about the two fields. A few, like the Cookmans, Barritts and Kemps, held their strips by right of freehold, but most were hereditary tenants of the lord of the manor, paying an annual copyhold rent of sixpence an acre to the recusant, Lord Dunbar at Burton Constable.

Regardless of status, the farmers of Owthorne worked together, and a strong spirit of co-operation prevailed. As a result, the community was largely self-sufficient. Generally speaking, some essential seeds and stock were obtained from the regular markets and fairs at Patrington and Hedon, but a journey across the frequently flooded plain of Holderness to the walled town of Hull, some twenty miles distant, was a rare event for the good folk of Owthorne.

The village by the sea consisted of twenty to thirty scattered cottages, a mill, the stone church and a large red-brick, thatched vicarage standing some eighty yards due west of the church. Of the hundred or so inhabitants, not all were engaged in husbandry. Four families, the Handsons, the Birds, Barkers and Dearloves, all went fishing, eking out meagre livings by daily excursions on the German Ocean in small boats launched from a sheltered creek to the north of the village, near Tunstall. William Sowarsby rented the mill and supplemented his living as a miller by running a bakery. Similarly, Tom Galloway combined the trades of shoemaking and keeping a beer-house. Tom Fewson was a time-served cooper and worked closely with Tom Gray, the village carpenter. In a more domestic field, Samuel Owbridge was a tailor, and Widow Preston sold most things from candles to cornplasters from the front room of her tiny cottage.

Standing proud above the low, thatched cottages of the village was the vicarage. With no inn available, the vicarage served as the venue for the Owthorne manor courts. Of course, the lord of the manor never ventured to this remote part of his domain, but twice-yearly his under-steward, the Hedon lawyer Henry Waterland, came with his clerk to hold these sessions at the vicarage. These were busy times for the young attorney, with wills to be examined or written; parish officials to be appointed; rents to be collected and surrenders and admissions of manorial tenants to be drawn up in the precise way beloved by lawyers.

The vicarage was the home of the Reverend Mr Henock Sinclare, vicar of Owthorne. This learned gentleman was of solid Yorkshire stock, the second son of David and Lucy Sinclare from Kilham on the Wolds. The men of the Sinclare family followed a curious mixture of the plough and the cloth. Henock's father had been a well-to-do farmer, but when Henock was born he had been named after his uncle, the worthy vicar of New Malton in the North Riding.

Henock's father had been twice-married. His first wife Elizabeth died soon after marriage in child bed, but from a second marriage four children were born: a daughter Lucy, and three sons, George, Henock and Samuel, all arriving on this earth during the drab and troublesome Puritan days of the Commonwealth.

Henock clearly inherited the brains of the family. At the age of fourteen he had outgrown the teaching capabilities of the little school at Kilham and gained a valuable scholarship to St John's College at Cambridge. From that moment onwards there was never any doubt that he was destined to become a minister of the Church of England, as his uncle had done before. In Cambridge he avoided all the frivolities and excesses frequently indulged in by his fellow undergraduates. A serious and conscientious student, Henock emerged from the university with a degree of Master of the Arts. In December 1679 he was ordained at York Minster by the Archbishop, and three months later was presented to the living of Owthorne through the patronage of Sir Francis Fane, lord of the Manor of Kilham. For the now Reverend Mr Henock Sinclare, it was to prove his first and only clerical appointment.

In this year of 1708 Henock was over fifty years of age and had guided the spiritual welfare of the parish for the past twenty-seven years. In appearance he was of short stature and decidedly on the portly side. Size apart, a round face, steely blue eyes and a rather bulbous nose were his most prominent features. A life-long bachelor, he invariably exhibited a serious nature which solidly matched the sombre clerical attire he wore most days of the week outside the vicarage. Enveloping the generous frame of the vicar was a long, black woollen waistcoat, reaching down to his thighs and fastened vertically at the front by a vast number of buttons carved from bone, each one covered in black cloth. Over the waistcoat was worn a black, three-quarter length coat and matching breeches buttoned around the legs below the knees, adjoining long black stockings. The only relief permitted to this sombre garb was a modest white lace neckerchief tied at the throat. To complete the picture, he wore a black, tricorn hat perched squarely upon a rather unfashionable grey wig of horsehair which flowed freely from under the hat, over his ears and the back of his head.

In the absence of a squire, the parson assumed the undisputed position of a surrogate gentry figure in the parish. In this small and isolated world of South Holderness, the vicar was well aware of his own superiority and nurtured a strong feeling of self-importance. This feeling, coupled with a fragile control of his temper, had on more than one occasion left the man in an embarrassing situation. Only months previously, one such occasion arose after a serious altercation with a former servant, William Hutton. It appeared that the vicar had been dissatisfied with the servant's efforts at removing low-hanging branches from above the boundary fence of the churchyard. Already in an irritated state of mind, the vicar chanced to meet Hutton in the vicarage yard, where he demanded that the servant go back and complete the task to his satisfaction. Hutton, however, was in no mood to repeat the work, and told his master so in no uncertain terms, spicing his words with the odd profanity. To the vicar this was insolent behaviour of an unforgivable nature. Regrettably for both men, the circumstance of their meeting was unfortunate. At the time, the vicar was on his way to the stables and was carrying a horsewhip in his hand. In an explosion of rage, the vicar lashed the servant three or four times about the shoulders and ended the encounter by dismissing the servant on the spot.

William Hutton was not a man to suffer his pains in silence. Forthwith he took himself, and his bruised and bleeding shoulders off to see a magistrate at Hedon. There the Justice, with scant regard for the cleric's rank or status, bound over the vicar to keep the peace and issued a summons for him to appear to answer Hutton's charges at the next Quarter Sessions of the Riding at Beverley. The next few days witnessed Henock Sinclare seething with indignation, but wisely the other occupants at the vicarage maintained a strict silence concerning the affair.

It would be true to say that like most parsons of the day, Henock was a respected, if not a popular figure in the district. Few parsons could claim the privilege of being popular in an agricultural community, for even if a lay impropriator, John Little, demanded the tithes of corn at Owthorne, the vicar collected the Easter dues in accordance with the terms of an ancient terrier. Without fail every Easter, the vicar would sit at a large table by the church door and receive tuppence for every person over sixteen in the parish; thrupence for every servant; tuppence for every cow that had calved, and a number of other fines which custom had imposed over the centuries on the parishioners. The vicar, seemingly, knew everyone and what every perch of land the parish contained of recordable value.

But Henock Sinclare was true to his faith and calling. Had he not on his induction to St Peter's boldly written with a firm and flowing hand in the parish register that he espoused the Book of Common Prayer and the 39 Articles? To his lasting credit, and unlike many of his clerical contemporaries, he was not an avaricious man. He neither sought additional benefices nor prebends. In short, he was comfortably placed and satisfied with his portion in life, which comprised mainly inherited means supplemented by modest earnings from his church offices. Nevertheless, in spite of his own comfortable state, Henock was not unmindful of the needs of others. When the occasion arose, he would lend money to worthy parishioners who sought his help. Hence when Peter Bilton wanted to extend his barn or Richard Storey planned to buy two strips of land in the Northfield from his neighbour, it was to the vicarage they went, hat in hand, to borrow money. A simple hand written note in the vicar's day book usually sufficed to record the transaction, and he had no illusions concerning swift repayments, or for that matter ever demanded interest on the loan. For Henock, the presence of the debtor and his family in their box pew at St Peter's on a Sunday morning, acknowledged by an imperceptible nod of approval from the man in the pulpit, was all the immediate recompense required by the worthy vicar of Owthorne.

Aside from spiritual duties, no parishioner could accuse their vicar of being idle or indolent in temporal matters. In spite of his portly appearance, Henock was remarkably fit for his age and ailed little. Illness he considered to be a warning from the Almighty for past misdeeds and something to be thrown off with a firm resolve to lead a better and more God-fearing life in the future.

In a small way, Henock joined in with the common occupation of husbandry. Although the living enjoyed no benefit of glebe lands, he had charge of a smallholding of nearly two acres adjoining the vicarage. In addition, the vicar rented a close of land from old Lady Bernardiston, and another smaller area known as Mason Garth, from Lord Dunbar. On the common pasture, he fully exercised a right to several beast gates where his small herd of cattle grazed over the summer months. In fact, his inventory of animals consisted not only of cows and horses but also included oxen, sheep and pigs. To house his corn and store a multitude of farming implements from ploughs to hay wains, the vicar rented a fair-sized barn on the Waxholme road from Robert Coleman. Indeed, no villager could complain that their vicar was a drone. Quite apart from the personal care he gave to his four beehives in the kitchen garden, when the time came to cut the hay in June or later in August to gather up the harvest, the vicar and his servant would join in with the other villagers to store away God's bounty.

It was at these times that the vicar discarded the familiar clerical garb. In its place he wore brown breeches and a loose smock, similar to those worn by all other labourers in the Holderness fields. Finally, off came the black, tricorn hat and wig to be replaced by a broad-brimmed, round straw hat, mercifully protecting the reverend's bald head from the sun's rays.

The brunt of the vicar's daily farm work, however, was done by John Jordan, one of his churchwardens, who in turn had the services of young Will Fallowdown, an orphan whose parents had both died of the smallpox in that terrible summer of 1699, when the dreaded disease had afflicted many in the villages of South Holderness.

Jordan was indispensable to the vicar. He ploughed the land, planted and gathered in the crops, milked the cows, sheared the sheep in season and generally looked after all the vicar's animals, with the sole exception of the horses, which remained the care of Adam Alvin in the vicarage stables. In return, Jordan received wages of four pounds per year, a goodly allowance of milk, butter and cheese, and lived freely with his family and Will Fallowdown in a cottage near Waxholme which the vicar rented from Mr Francis Blunt.

There was one other service of an agricultural nature which the vicar performed annually for all the farmers of the parish. Over time it became the custom for him to ride out to Hedon, accompanied by a servant, to buy fresh seed corn at the Magdalen Fair, returning with full panniers hanging down from the flanks of the horses. On arrival, the waiting villagers would examine the vicar's purchases, share the cost and decide what was to be planted and where, for the coming year. In this simple and recurring way, the life of the parish, both spiritual and temporal, revolved around the church and the vicarage.

The vicarage itself was a half-timbered, red-bricked, thatched dwelling of great antiquity. Some said it had been built by monks from Kirkstall Abbey, to act as a lodge and stables soon after that abbey had expropriated the church from their French counterparts who had been expelled from Burstall Priory. Whatever the origins of the house, there was no doubt that it was by far the largest and oldest building in the village, its walls bearing visible marks of fearful and furious storms. The building consisted of three bays with a kitchen, a living-room and a parlour on the ground floor. Leading off from the parlour the vicar had built on a small extension which served as his private study and also housed a library of books, a collection of volumes mainly on religious themes, willed to him by his uncle Henock at Malton. Two butteries led off from the kitchen, places where the beer was brewed and provisions stored. The whole was

6

floored with red-brick and the inner walls plastered and smoothed over from countless coats of limewash. A single wooden staircase off the living-room gave access to a landing and to four chambers which served as bedrooms and completed the inventory of useable rooms inside the building.

Out by the kitchen door and across a squarish yard, was situated a long, thatched stable block. Inside, in a row, were a number of stalls where the vicar's horses were stabled, whilst above and reached by broad wooden stairs, the roof space housed much of the tackle required for the horses, the oxen and the wains. At one end of this space were found the quarters of the vicar's servant, Adam Alvin. Immediately to the south of the stables was the kitchen garden. Extending to a little over one acre in size, it served both as an ornamental floral area and a source of fruit and vegetables for the household. It was here that the vicar lovingly tended his beehives.

Apart from the vicar, the household consisted of his two nieces, Mary and Catherine Sinclare, Adam Alvin, his manservant and general handyman, and a young female servant, Sarah Handson, the daughter of John Handson, a widower of Waxholme. The two nieces had lived with their uncle for as long as they could remember and all attempts by the elder girl, Mary, to discuss details of their parentage from their guardian had met with only abrupt and meagre replies. Their mother had apparently died giving birth to the younger sister Catherine, and their father, the vicar's brother Samuel, had left Kilham to seek his fortune in the Americas and had not been seen or heard of since.

The two girls differed both in appearance and character. Mary Sinclare was about twenty-five years of age, strong in will and body, with dark hair and brown eyes standing out in sharp contrast to her pale skin and full red lips. Mary looked after the running of the household. She ordered the provisions, supervised the malting of the barley for beer making, salted beef or cured hams, taking good care that they were kept in order of age on rows of black iron hooks which hung down from the ceiling in the long kitchen. She supervised Sarah, a slip of a girl barely twelve years old, who had been taken on by her uncle only the year before, mainly out of charity to help the girl's father, who had fallen on hard times. Mary also saw to the basket of bread, cheese and ale carried out to John Jordan and Will Fallowdown in the fields at ten o'clock every day of the week except on the Lord's day. There were herbs to be planted, vegetables to be collected from the kitchen garden, and a host of other domestic duties to be done which formed the routine of Mary's daily chores.

Whilst Mary performed her duties well in Owthorne's scene of isolated tranquillity, she constantly suffered from an inner restlessness. Although she regularly gave thanks to God for the comforts she and her sister received at the vicarage and for the kind patronage of their uncle, she brooded in the silence about her future state. Of course, she loved her sister deeply and cared for her when she was ill, but the thought of remaining in her present situation, destined to remain an old maid, without a husband's love, children and external happiness, filled her with despair. As the Holderness seasons came and went with dull and inevitable monotony, Mary fretted as to how she could escape from these rural surroundings which imprisoned her as surely as some town prison. How could she achieve the intimacy of her desires? Where could she find true love and happiness with a man of her choice and bear his children? It all seemed an impossible dream in her current situation.

Mary's sister Catherine, by contrast, was small of stature and slim of build. She did not enjoy the same robust constitution as her sister. Pale in complexion and gaunt looking, she had suffered from coughing and fainting fits since childhood. These attacks she strove to suffer in silence, almost choking on occasions during her uncle's sermons rather than interrupt the flow of pious words with her hoarse, high-pitched coughing. Catherine sought solace and a remedy for her affliction in the village, but sadly all the potions offered by Widow Preston were to no avail. In desperation she had experimented with thick and vile-looking concoctions peddled by passing gypsies, but alas, these too proved to be as ineffective as Widow Preston's brews.

Catherine's plight was cruelly ignored by her uncle, who roughly brushed aside all pleas from the two nieces that Catherine should seek help from a 'proper' apothecary at Hedon or Hull.

In recognition of her inferior status, Catherine was relegated to the service of make do and mend. All their clothes, the household and church linen were in her care, and in this area she showed admirable skill. Even her demanding uncle could find no fault with the quality of her work. As a result all but the very largest items of heavy clothing were made at the vicarage. To Catherine also fell the task of cleaning and decorating the church in readiness for the whole parish to enter by the south door on Sunday morning, to sit and listen to the usual lengthy and heavy homily on God's goodness and man's ingratitude from her uncle.

Apart from Sarah, the young servant girl, the only other resident at the vicarage was Adam Alvin, the vicar's servant and general handyman about the house. Adam's arrival at Owthorne was regarded as an act of providence. Some twenty years before, in a terrible storm at sea, a ship had foundered in the shallows of the German Ocean, off Owthorne. That night, a spar from the wreck was washed up on the beach. Clinging to the spar was a woman, and when the watching villagers dashed across the shingle to rescue her, they were amazed to find that the poor woman was clutching an infant in her arms, protecting it with all her remaining strength against the force of the waves. The woman did not long survive her ordeal and expired within minutes, but the baby seemed little the worse for its terrible adventure. As there were no other survivors from the wreck, it was impossible to throw any light on the identity or origin of the baby, so a problem arose as to what to do with the tiny boy. None of the parishioners wanted to take in the child, and the vicar, believing that its safe arrival was a sure sign from God, shrank from sending him to the poorhouse, and instead had the boy brought up at the vicarage.

One or two weeks after the baby's uninvited arrival, the vicar decided that it was his Christian duty to have the baby baptised. This ceremony of necessity brought forward the question of what the child was to be called. For the Christian name, the vicar simply chose Adam, the first man of creation. The surname was more problematical, but as the villagers had by this time discovered that the ship which foundered on their coastline was 'The Alvin', so the child was given this name. It was to be a name still remembered in those parts three hundred years later.

As time went by, Adam was given the rudiments of reading and writing at the vicarage. In return he was obliged to carry out all the menial jobs about the household and yard. It might have been expected by those who knew of the circumstances of Adam's arrival at Owthorne that the young man would show some mark of gratitude for his good fortune and for receiving the basic necessities of life. In fact, he grew up to be a moody youth, with a morose and sullen disposition. As the years progressed he felt a growing sense of resentment about his life of servitude and lowly station in life. To all outside the vicarage his manner was brusque and he made no friends. Even Will Fallowdown, who was of comparable age and with whom he was in daily contact, could find no point of comradeship. In this self-imposed isolated existence Adam Alvin exhibited all the unhappy characteristics of a loner, without any redeeming graces, even of a most rustic nature.

For the village and the villagers, Adam felt nothing but distaste, and inwardly he cherished a longing to break away from the rural monotony of his enforced station. Only when he was busy around the stables working with the horses did any spark of interest or enthusiasm kindle within him. In this field, he had undoubted skills, for he seemed to understand the moods and ways of these animals to an extraordinary degree. He regularly exercised the vicar's horses, riding along the cliff paths between Tunstall and Holmpton, when he would feel exhilarated by a combination of the speed of the gallop and the noise of the constant crashing of the waves upon the shores.

Adam's desire to leave Owthorne was heightened every time he accompanied his master on a journey to the town of Hull. On these occasions, whilst the vicar took his victuals and rest at the King's Head in the High Street, Adam would slip away by the inn's side passage and spend an hour listening to the mariners on the quayside. Stories were heard of the great city of London, of Hamburg across the ocean and wondrous tales of voyages on the Russian seas, with descriptions of amazing showers of brightly-coloured lights in the sky. These tales only served to give Adam a lust for freedom and adventure, coupled with a reciprocal dissatisfaction for his own humdrum way of life. Only one thing held him back from escaping his rural prison. For a long time, Adam had nurtured a deep passion for Mary Sinclare, and to his unbounded joy, Mary showed signs of returning his affection.

These mutual feelings of love were not the result of some sudden outburst of passion but had matured slowly over time. In days gone by Mary had shown a fleeting interest in John Pighills junior, the son of the rector of Patrington. Sadly, this young man quickly acquired a reputation for being an inveterate womaniser and a drunkard about the taverns of Hull. After a short while, both parties lost all interest in each other.

'The children never know what's good for them,' the rector said philosophically. 'Time may yet prove a long shot from Cupid's bow.' He would then sigh and push forward a bottle of brandy in the direction of his good friend Henock Sinclare, ready to change the subject of their conversation to more convivial matters.

Following the debacle of the unsuccessful courtship with John Pighills, Mary was unable to find another man to further her search for a possible husband. Indeed, even her socialising in the neighbourhood was a strictly limited activity. The sisters habitually accompanied their uncle on his regular visits to the Patrington rectory, where they enjoyed the female company of the rector's wife, Phyllis. More enjoyable still were their outings to see the young Dunn family at the Manor House at Patrington. Days would go by and often stretch into weeks when Mary and Catherine never left the confines of their small village, except on visits of Christian charity to give alms to the parish needy, or to exercise the horses along the coastal paths by Waxholme and Tunstall. Catherine found riding a strain on her weak frame and rarely ventured in the saddle, but Mary was an excellent horsewoman.

For safety's sake, her uncle always insisted that Adam accompanied Mary on her rides. Mary soon began to admire the skill of the servant in his handling of the horses and grew to enjoy their outings together. For his part, Adam relished the attention paid to him by Mary, and to her, and her alone, his customary brusque and churlish manner softened. He eagerly looked forward to the times they would spend together in the saddle, or back in the stables brushing down and grooming the animals. Horse-riding apart, Mary encouraged Adam to keep up with his reading, and they regularly shared books she had borrowed from her friends at Patrington. In the evenings, after supper, they would sit un-chaperoned by either Mary's uncle or sister in the kitchen of the vicarage, taking turns to read aloud passages from the latest book. At times Mary would gently guide Adam through hesitations over difficult words, and at the end they would converse in an animated fashion about the themes and stories that they had just read together.

These regular meetings, aided by the remote surroundings of their existence, inevitably planted a seed of mutual affection. At first, Mary's feelings were restricted to an innocent admiration for Adam's manly appearance; his tall stature, broad shoulders and handsome dark features, which contrasted so sharply with his eyes of bright blue. Inevitably, the initial admiration developed into stirrings of affection and from affection to a heated passion. For his part, as a man starved of love, or indeed kindness, Adam did not hesitate to respond to Mary's advances with eager expressions of a similar nature.

Chapter Two

Even the most naïve soul in the village could have told the young couple that their desired union would receive no blessing from the spiritual guardian of the parish. Adam's first tentative declaration of their mutual feelings of love were greeted by a sudden and violent outburst from the vicar.

'The Devil you do!' shouted the affronted parson. 'You dare to come to me with such foolery. I who brought you up from nothing. Know your station and forget it not.'

Crushed and thoroughly dejected, Adam slunk back to the stables, there to harbour bitter thoughts about his master. For days afterwards Henock Sinclare and his two nieces supped together in silence, until at last the vicar regained his composure.

In truth, the vicar's objection to the match was not merely based on a question of breeding or class. There was also an inherent selfishness in the man, who enjoyed a comfortable mode of living and was unwilling to endanger this convenient and pleasant way of life. To the question of class the vicar might well have admitted openly, if pressed to the point; the second reason he would probably not even have recognised in himself, or if at all, would never have confessed it to another living soul. The vicar was easily deluded by his own reasoning. Mindful of Mary's earlier brief attachment to the young John Pighills, he soon persuaded himself that such amorous leanings were only to be expected in a woman entering into a state of maturity. A great wave of satisfaction flooded through him with the thought that, as Mary's legal guardian, he had acted wisely in rejecting Adam's suit, thus helping Mary to avoid another gross error of judgement. Unfortunately, if the Pighills episode had been of the nature of a minor disturbance to all the parties concerned, the vicar grossly underestimated the effect on Adam and Mary of his refusal to give consent to their union. Adam never recovered from this rebuff, and from then on a smouldering fire of hate grew in his heart and slowly began to consume him with bitter resentment.

One summer's day in June Adam was ordered to accompany his master on a journey to go to the Hull market. On their way, the vicar's main thoughts were concerned with the task ahead, namely to purchase four good milk cows to augment the village stock. A few paces behind the vicar rode his sullen servant, who held no such thoughts of the job in hand but stared vacantly at the back of the object of his loathing.

The journey to Hull proved to be remarkably easy. Little rain had fallen over the early days of the month, and the often impassable areas by Keyingham Marsh were of no consequence to the two experienced riders. A brief stop at the Hall in Hedon found the Waterlands away from home, but a welcome cup of ale brought out from the kitchen revived the travellers and set them on their way. In turn, they passed through Preston, Bilton, Summergangs, and after crossing the wooden beams at the North Bridge, they entered into Hull. The vicar had arranged for their overnight stay at the King's Head, ready for an early appearance at the market in the morning. That evening, with time on his hands, the vicar sought company in kind at the house of Robert Banks, the vicar of Holy Trinity church. Mr Sinclare was not disappointed with the hospitality he received from his clerical colleague, and returned to the inn at a late hour under the protection of a burly night watchman.

Adam's movements did not vary from his customary habit. After seeing to the horses and taking a bite to eat in the rear quarters of the inn, he drifted to the river quayside and idly paced the wooden boards seeking out, but not greatly expecting to see, a familiar face among the seated sailors. As he walked, his solitude was broken by a voice from behind.

'Noo then, 'ere's a likely lad.'

Adam turned instantly to look into the face of a tanned mariner, who was leaning easily on a warehouse wall.

'Looking fer worr'ck?' the man asked, drawing deeply on a short clay pipe and blowing a haze of grey smoke in Adam's general direction.

'No,' Adam replied cautiously. 'I'm in service.'

The seaman persisted. 'So was I, boy, so was I, 'til I 'ad m'callin'. It's a man's life afloat and I cud use a lad like you. Why don't you look her ovver? Aint she a beaut'?'

'Beautiful' was probably the last word Adam would have used to describe the moored, black barge which seemed to correspond to the area vaguely indicated by the pipe stem of the mariner. Curiosity conquered the mistrust, however, and after a moment's hesitation Adam climbed down the rungs of a rope ladder, crossed over the deck and disappeared into the bowels of the vessel. A tankard of thick, strong ale drawn from a large brown pot standing in the corner of the cramped cabin soon appeared in his hand, and the master of the vessel, for such was the pipe smoker, began to tell Adam of his voyages carrying lead ingots from Derbyshire along the Yorkshire rivers and out to sea to London. The master enticingly spoke of that big city with its fine gentry, its clever rogues and all the hustle and bustle that made Hull seem pale and insignificant in comparison. At times, the master took his craft across the sea to land the metal at the port of Amsterdam, where fair-haired maids in white billowing bonnets, coloured aprons and wooden clogs clacked along the cobble-stoned quaysides selling herrings and blue china dogs.

'I done well in the trade,' the master continued. 'Very well indeed, so I just bought another boat. She's being fitted out in a yard at Paull. Won't be long afore she's ready to sail.'

At that point, a second man appeared in the cabin. 'This 'ere's m'brother Tom,' said the master. 'He'll tek on the new boat and 'e'll need a man such as you to crew.'

'That's right,' Tom said. 'But who are you?'

'My name's Adam Alvin and I come from Owthorne near the sea.'

Tom sniffed suspiciously and helped himself to a tankard of ale from the pot. 'You in trouble?' he asked, looking at Adam suspiciously.

'No,' Adam replied, drawing himself up in an obvious show of self-righteousness.

'Adam 'ere 'll 'mek a fine crewman,' the master interrupted swiftly. 'Look 'ere, we sails on the morning tide and two weeks from now we'll be good and ready to work with both craft. We cud do with you alongside. What d'you say?'

Thwarted in love and downcast in spirit, Adam could not believe his good fortune. At a stroke he would break free from the chains of despised servitude, and visions floated before him of untold adventures at sea. Nevertheless, and in spite of all his inward excitement, Adam had the good sense to ask the master the terms of his new employment.

'I can do any job you want on this boat,' Adam said boldly. 'But what do I get for m'pains?'

'We pays the goin' rate 'ereabouts,' the master answered. 'Eight pence a day and all your victuals. If we does well on a trip there could be some pickin's to be 'ad, but that's as may be.'

'It don't sound much to me,' Adam said cautiously. 'I'd expected it to be a shilling.'

'You'll do no better in these parts, I'll wager that,' Tom added. 'You'll be tret fair by us. Everybody in this port knows the Bolger brothers fer fair dealings.'

Adam soon convinced himself that the offered terms were no worse than the dole he received at the vicarage.

'So be it, then,' said Adam, and he shook hands with the two men. 'Rest assured, two weeks from today I'll be good and ready, waiting on this quayside.'

Adam returned to the inn. It was difficult for the young man to contain his excitement. Even the normally wearisome journey back, forcing four unwilling beasts moving at snail's pace onwards towards the village by the sea, passed as though in a dream for the distracted servant. He smelt the sea breeze in his nostrils as he had never done before, and the cries of the seabirds suddenly became a signal heralding a new calling. It was a romance of a very different nature which now monopolised his thoughts, and even the commonplace movement of his body in the saddle was translated mentally into a rhythmic rise and fall of standing on some deck far out at sea.

Eventually the ill-matched pair of riders and the beasts reached their destination and turned into the stable yard of the vicarage. Whilst the vicar and a group of locals were busy looking over the new purchases, Adam lost no time entering the house to tell Mary of his new plans.

In relating to Mary what had been agreed on the riverside at Hull, Adam had neither the understanding nor a thought of how devastating hearing his words would be to her. It was a lesson painfully learned, for it seemed to him that a verbal volcano had erupted and showered him with a burning lava of furious and angry words.

'You would leave me in this God-forsaken place with false promises to return. Am I to become an old maid here and wait for ever? You heartless man, full of empty words. Is there no love in your heart for me?'

Adam, taken aback by the ferocity of Mary's outburst, collapsed on a nearby chair, holding his head in his hands.

'What can we do?' he said in a miserable tone. 'Of course I love you and want you to be my wife, but what can we do when that old fool won't hear of us being wed?'

Mary's anger subsided as she stood over the disconsolate figure. Always a more determined and practical person, her mind raced through possible ways to end their dilemma. After a few moments' thought, she placed her hands firmly on Adam's shoulders.

'I know what's to do,' she said at last. 'I'm going to ask him myself. After all we've done for him, he's not to refuse me, just you wait and see, dearest. We'll wed soon enough, to be sure.'

Mary pulled Adam to his feet and brushed his hands from his face with her own.

'Never fear, I'm not losing you to some leaky old barge in the river,' she said with a laugh.

Adam did not join in with Mary's laughter. Inwardly he still felt miserable that his dream of escaping from the vicarage had been broken. Mary, however, was determined to carry out her plan and would brook no further dissent. She ended the interview by giving Adam a firm kiss and a pat on the rump to propel him out of the house.

* * * * *

After his exertions in St Peter's on the Lord's Day, Henock Sinclare always insisted on Monday's dinner being the main meal of the week. This took place with rigid punctuality in the afternoon at three o'clock. Supervised closely by Mary, Sarah would turn the spit mechanism in the fireplace of the kitchen to ensure that the roast was done to the vicar's liking. At the appointed time, he would be summoned to address the joint, now lying on a large pewter platter, to carve large pieces of meat for himself and his two nieces. When thanks had been given to the Almighty, the three would eat their meal.

After the meal it was customary for Henock to retire to his study to await Mary bringing him some additional treat to enjoy in quiet surroundings. Similarly, Catherine would go straight back to her bedroom, whilst Mary saw that Sarah and Adam were fed in their turn from the roast meat and left-over vegetables.

On that warm June afternoon nothing appeared to be out of the ordinary. Adam, who knew of Mary's important mission, ate in silence, ignoring Sarah's excited chatter, relaying to Mary all the gossip the young girl had gleaned from other villagers after the Sunday service. With a full stomach, Adam pushed his chair back from the table. He gave a low grunt of thanks in Mary's direction, and after giving her a knowing nod, he left the kitchen to go back to the stables.

As Sarah busied herself clearing the table and putting the plates to wash, Mary cut some wedges of fresh bread and cheese. Arranging the pieces neatly on a plate, she approached the study door, paused, drew a deep breath, knocked on the door and entered.

'I've brought you some of our best cheese, uncle,' she announced.

Henock beamed. 'You are a good girl! I don't know what I'd do without you.'

Mary frowned. This was the very last sort of compliment she wished to hear at this time. She moved quickly over to the sideboard. 'A glass of port wine?' she said, and without waiting for an answer poured out a measure from a bottle.

Henock beamed again and gave a simple gesture of acceptance. 'Much obliged,' he said.

'Uncle, may I have a word with you?'

'Of course, my dear. Pray sit down. Whatever is it that couldn't be said at table?'

Mary sat down and began a much rehearsed dialogue with as much confidence as she could muster.

'Uncle, I know that you are always solicitous in seeking great happiness for Catherine and myself.'

'Quite so,' said Henock, his eyes barely lifting from the plate of food before him.

'Also, you know of Adam's great loyalty to our family.'

'A trifling headstrong at times,' the vicar interposed. 'But I cannot complain of his work with the horses.'

Mary felt uneasy. The conversation was not progressing quite as she had hoped and she quickly decided that a more direct approach was necessary.

'You know, uncle, some time ago Adam asked for my hand in marriage.'

For the first time, Mary secured the full attention of her uncle. He looked hard at Mary. 'Just so,' he said quizzically, and waited for Mary to continue.

'Well,' she said. 'It would give me the greatest happiness to marry Adam, and we wish to have your blessing.'

Henock pushed way his plate. 'This is just tomfoolery!' He almost shouted the words. 'The boy's a foundling. How could you ever consider making such a match? It would be a disgrace to us all, here and at Kilham. I cannot agree to such a ridiculous union.'

Mary felt crushed and showed obvious signs of distress. Even Henock could not help but see the effect his words had on his now distraught niece. Calming himself, he made some attempt to soften the blow.

'My dear, of course, I'm not against you finding a suitable husband. Although I'm a bachelor myself, I recognise the holy state of matrimony. As you say, I have only your happiness at heart, but we must find you a suitable match, mustn't we? Not a servant, eh?'

Mary tried her hardest to force back tears. She recognised the utter failure of her mission and rose to go. 'Thank you' would have been the obvious words of ending the meeting, but she could not bring herself to say such useless and insincere words. Turning, she left the study with tears welling up in her eyes.

Leaving the house, Mary fled towards the stables. Once inside she saw Adam in one of the horse boxes. Falling into his arms, she buried her head in his chest and cried convulsively. There was no need for Adam to ask what had taken place in the study. All too clearly he could see that Mary had fared no better with her uncle than he had done previously.

Adam did his best to soothe Mary, but it was to no avail. As he held her in his arms, he felt trapped like a rabbit in a snare, desperate to be free. On one hand, Mary would not let him go to sea, whilst on the other, he could not marry without his master's permission.

''ush, girl, 'ush,' he said softly. 'D'you want the 'ole village t'ear you sobbin'?'

Mary looked up at Adam piteously.

'What's to be done?' she pleaded. 'What can we do? If we run away, uncle would send word and no minister would marry us.'

Adam paused. He could not remember another time that Mary had asked him for guidance on any matter unconnected with his work in the stables.

'Maybe you should let me try m'hand at sea for a while,' he said. 'When I mek good and 'ave some money in m'pocket, I'll be back and we can be wed.'

'Leave me here alone!' Mary cried out. 'Are you such a coward as to run away for fear of a parson?'

Adam took a deep breath. Until now he had thought that Mary's emotional state was only to be expected from a distraught woman frustrated in her desire for love and marriage. Now she questioned his courage, and his manly pride was deeply wounded.

He looked around to see that they were alone in the stables.

'If needs be, shall we rid ourselves of your uncle?'

Mary looked at Adam in astonishment and stopped crying. 'Do you mean kill him?' Her voice faltered in a wave of uncertainty.

'Aye, do away w'him, if we 'ave to,' was the reply.

There was a moment's silence, then Mary whispered a single word. 'Yes.' It was as if some other person had spoken the word, although she herself had meant to say nothing.

'Yes, yes, yes,' she repeated mechanically. 'It's the only way we can be together and be happy.'

Adam felt his confidence returning.

'Then it must be done quick,' he said in a low voice. 'Get Sarah out o' the way. Send 'er off packing 'ome. But what's to be done with your sister?'

'She'll help us,' Mary replied. She's nothing to thank uncle for. I'll make her swear to stay silent and she'll do what I tell her to do. Leave Catherine to me.'

Later that evening Mary invented an excuse to go out of the house to see Adam. Alone in the stables, they formulated their evil plan.

Chapter Three

The following day Sarah could not believe her unexpected good fortune at being sent home on an errand.

'Give your father this letter and say he's to come and see Mr Sinclare directly after service time on Sunday,' Mary ordered. 'Take care to go straight home and do not tarry on the roadside.'

Mary gave the young girl a small parcel of bread and cheese for the journey and gently bundled her out of the house.

'Mind you're back by noon tomorrow,' were the last words she heard from her mistress as she happily went on her way up the winding lane which led to Waxholme.

If the removal of Sarah was a problem soon solved, Catherine, normally so compliant to all Mary's wishes, proved to be a more reluctant accomplice. Although she felt few feelings of love or affection for her guardian, he did not appear in her eyes as Mary portrayed, a merciless tyrant. Hard and selfish perhaps, but not a person to deserve such a heinous punishment. At the same time, she understood only too well her sister's desperate situation. Catherine clearly remembered her own feelings of rejection in the past when she had made excursions to Widow Preston's on the excuse to buy thread, but in truth to try out some new remedy for her cough. On the way she loitered shamelessly, watching out for a glimpse of any young man of the village. When the occasion arose, she never hesitated to use some artless deception, such as crossing the road, contrived collisions at corners, dropping articles, or some other artifice to engineer contact with some young, ruddy-cheeked farmhand who had taken her fancy. If successful, Catherine then tried to look demure and feigned a pose of maidenly helplessness. The result was always the same. A hurried apology and gruff 'Mornin', miss,' as befitted the station of the vicar's niece, whereupon the sturdy lad would hurry away, leaving Catherine to continue on to Widow Preston's with a pounding heart and often an uncontrolled fit of coughing. The bitter truth was plain to see. Catherine was destined to remain a spinster all her life.

In her imprisoned world, Catherine had in Mary the only person in whom she could confide her innermost thoughts and longings. In return, she maintained a fierce loyalty to her sister, which bound the two closely together.

'Believe me, sister dear,' Mary said. 'We shall try once more to get uncle to relent and give us his blessing, but I fear he will be obdurate and we shall be forced to take this terrible path. Rest assured, we do not do this willingly.'

'Surely there must be some other way,' Catherine countered. 'Why can you not go to Mr Pighills at Patrington and get him to marry you? Once done and you're married, it cannot be undone.'

'You know full well, Catherine, Mr Pighills would never consent to marry us. He'd talk to uncle and that would be the end of it.'

Mary looked hard at her sister. Now in desperate straights, her voice took on a pleading tone.

'You need do nothing to promote this terrible deed. All I ask you to do, if you love me, is to swear an oath on the Holy Bible, that you will never tell a living soul about what will happen. That's all I ask of you.'

It was this bond of sisterly love which made Catherine's doubts seem less important. Slowly and reluctantly she gave way to Mary's desperate pleadings. In some muddled way, Catherine began to imagine that the death of her uncle would end for ever the daily drudgery of her own life; the endless make do and mend and seeing to the needs of that dreary church. She stared at the drawn face of her sister, saw her colourless cheeks, and above all, the eyes which seemed to beg for approval. At last, Catherine surrendered with a barely audible voice of assent and collapsed upon the shoulders of her sister, giving way to floods of tears.

The promise was made. A wave of relief drenched through Mary's entire body, and with the force of Catherine's head thrown upon her, they fell back on Catherine's bed, the two sisters locked in an emotional embrace. Mary soon regained her composure, however, and with typical determination she took control of the situation.

'Sister dear, you must swear that oath never to tell a living soul of what will happen – till death.'

Catherine did not reply, but whilst she continued to sigh and sob, Mary quickly crossed the room, seized her sister's bible and returned to the figure on the bed. In the fading light of that June evening, the macabre scene in the bedroom drew to its close; Catherine's white fingers held down by Mary's firm hand across the leather cover of the bible, her lips barely moving to repeat the words her sister recited. It was as though the instrument of God was being used to do the Devil's work.

Satisfied the deed to be done would remain for ever a secret within the walls of the vicarage, Mary put down the bible, kissed Catherine and left the bedroom. Leaving the house she entered the stables and found Adam busy with the horses.

''Tis done dearest,' she said. 'Catherine has sworn on the bible She'll keep our secret, to be sure, so there's nothing to stop us now. When can it be done?'

'Best do it quick,' Adam replied. ''e's over at Coleman's 'aggling over the beasts we brought back from 'ull. I'll see 'im when 'e gets back and do 'im in for good.'

Adam waited for Mary to react to his words. Perhaps she would show some sign of wanting to draw back from the deed they had planned together, but Mary gave no hint of retraction or remorse.

'Good,' she said firmly. 'Let it be done quickly.'

* * * * *

As the early evening sun lowered in the sky, Henock entered the vicarage yard by the back gate. He was in a foul temper, and as he marched to the house his shoes sent the loose gravel flying in all directions. At that moment, the sheer ingratitude and perversity of some of the parish farmers occupied all this thoughts. Far from being pleased with the parson's efforts in purchasing and delivering safely the four beasts, a few had had the temerity not only to criticise the quality of the animals, but had also refused point blank to share in the cost. Unaccustomed to such a rebuke, the vicar had lost his temper, and it had taken cooler heads some time to forge an agreed settlement. Tired and irritable, the vicar made for the house, but half-way across the yard he was intercepted by Adam blocking his path. Henock noted with detached surprise that Adam was carrying a spade in his right hand.

'Reverend, a word if you please.'

'Not now, Adam, not now,' the vicar replied testily, and continued in the direction of the kitchen door, holding forward a hand as if to part some insignificant and imaginary barrier. In a second the invisible became particularly visible as Adam moved into the path of the vicar.

'It can't wait,' Adam said gruffly. 'I want to marry your Mary. M'mind's made up. I'll not stand any delay.'

The vicar stopped in his tracks, for a moment speechless. This new, unexpected onslaught, coming as it did, soon after the affair of the cows, was more than his equilibrium could bear. Clenching his fists, he swung an arm forward to menace the face of the demanding servant.

'Damn you!' he roared. 'Damn your insolence and get you gone this instant or I'll fetch my whip to you.'

'The Dev'l take you,' snarled Adam, taking a quick pace backward. Swinging the spade from behind and over his head, he brought it crashing down on the vicar's head. For one horrible moment nothing happened. Instead of falling down as his assailant imagined, the victim remained standing, swaying slightly with a bewildered expression upon his face; his eyes were glazed and the hands, which moments before had been closed in a belligerent pose, now opened and made as if to reach up and straighten the broad-brimmed hat which was now cocked at a foolish angle upon his head. The hands never reached the hat, for Adam struck again in blind fury, this time bringing Henock to his knees with a heavy groan. Even so, life still persisted. In a final act, the victim's hands grasped the coarse cloth of Adam's breeches in a last desperate attempt to pull himself up and out of the range of the murderous blows. Breaking free, Adam raised the spade one more time until the blade was level with his own face. He brought the weapon down with a terrible force, the metal cleaving through the unprotected skull with a sickening, cracking sound. The lifeless corpse crumpled noiselessly on the gravel at the feet of his assassin. Adam stared at the prone form, but seemed powerless to move as the spade slipped from his grasp, sliding across the prone body and coming to rest on the ground. Trembling in all his limbs, only with the greatest of efforts did he turn away from the victim and notice the two sisters staring in horror at the scene from the open kitchen door.

After a moment's hesitation, Mary left her sister in the doorway and hurried over to the two motionless figures in the yard. Putting a firm hand on Adam's shoulder, her steady words brought the dazed man back to reality.

''Tis done now, and well he deserved it. Be quick, there's no time to lose; you must hide all traces and leave nothing to chance. Take up your spade and dig deep – deeper than any dog can uncover. Do you hear me?'

Adam gathered his wits about him, reassured by the calm delivery of Mary's words. 'Leave it to me. I'll do it,' he replied. 'Take th'sens off to the Barritts.'

Mary, sure now that Adam was in command of his senses, needed no second bidding to leave the scene of death. The sisters took one last look at the lifeless form of their uncle and escaped from the scene into the vicarage. Within minutes both women were walking, at first with faltering, but then with evermore determined steps, to the east end of the village to pay an unannounced call on old Mrs Barritt.

Fear of being disturbed at his work made Adam dig furiously. The top layer of gravel and the crust of dark rich soil soon gave way to heavy, yellow clay. It was now growing dark, and as dusk began to shroud the scene of the crime, the half-light seemed to give an impetus to the work of the sweating servant. At last he was satisfied with the size of the hole, and seizing his late master by the feet, he dragged the heavy body into the makeshift grave. Pausing briefly to wipe sweat from his brow, Adam reflected with cruel humour that for a man who had presided with much ceremony at many a village burial, his own was in stark contrast.

'Good ridd'nce,' was the brief parting prayer from the hot and sticky man as he paused to toss into the grave the vicar's crumpled and blood-stained hat.

Adam carefully covered the body with clods of clay, then the soil and finally a few shovels of gravel to return the contours of the yard to its former appearance. Moments later he crossed the yard and reached the pump. Giving the handle a few vigorous pulls, he cooled himself under the gushing spout. Finally, taking great care to remove the mud which spattered his boots, he entered the kitchen and made a path directly to the late vicar's study. It was dark inside the room, but Adam needed no candle. Throwing open the shutters, faint light from the moon provided all the illumination he required. Standing on a long sideboard was the fat, green, onion-shaped bottle of the vicar's finest port. The cork jumped from the bottle's neck with a reassuring report, and almost in a single movement Adam collapsed backwards into a large padded armchair, threw his head back and gulped down the wine to the last comforting drop. At length, gasping for breath, he looked about him at the familiar surroundings, picking out in the reflected light the pieces of furniture and ornaments that decorated the working room of the late incumbent of Owthorne. In Adam's face could be detected an unmistakable glow of triumph. The worst was over, he told himself, and a warm feeling of confidence surged in his whole body as the red wine began to take effect.

With an effort Adam rose, pushed the chair away and retraced his footsteps to the stables. On the way he lit a lantern and collected a bundle of old corn sacks, one of the vicar's wigs and his horsewhip, items which Mary had carefully placed near the back door. Inside the stables the vicar's favourite horse occupied the first box. Adam hung the lantern on a hook above the opening and began the task of strapping on the saddle and bridle. This done, he knelt down on the stone flags beside the animal and started forcing a sack upon one of its front legs. The horse, unaccustomed to such treatment, tried to draw back and pull its leg free.

"'odd 'ard!' muttered Adam, persevering in his work until he had the mare ready, strangely shod with four sacks, one tied to each leg. It was then the turn of his own horse, standing in the end box quietly engaged in munching at a pile of hay, little suspecting that more service would be forced upon it at such a late hour. In half the time taken with the first animal, he saddled and muffled the hooves of the second horse and led them both out of the yard into the deserted roadway. The moonlight which had earlier aided his work now caused him to curse and wish that clouds would come to blot out his movements. Adam mounted his horse, and pulling at the bridle of the second animal, he set out on his journey in the direction of Holmpton village.

The moonlight soon began to play tricks. The sudden scurry of a fox darting across his path caused Adam to rein in his horse, and brought a moment of panic to the man. The incident made him acutely aware of the danger of being recognised by some chance encounter on the road. After all that he had accomplished earlier, he mused, it was too much to risk, and with a deft movement he forced the horses off the road and across the open fields and meadows. The padded hooves pounded steadily on until Adam judged he was close to Holmpton. Reaching a secluded spot by the cliff edge, he dismounted, and tied his own horse to a nearby gatepost. Quickly he tore away the sacking from the hooves of the vicar's horse, gave the animal a sharp slap on the rump, and sent it ambling away into the black of the night. From his saddlebag, Adam removed the vicar's wig and riding whip. Noting in the moonlight the crumpled state of the cliff at that point, he threw the objects over the edge, but took care that they would not be in danger of being washed away by the tide.

The homeward ride proved to be no less nerve-racking than the journey out. On reaching the low-built cottages of Owthorne, within a mere hundred yards or so of the vicarage, Adam spotted some dark figures walking on the road ahead. Jerking his horse off the road to a standstill under the comforting low branches of a tree, he strained to see who these unwelcome intruders were. For what seemed an eternity, the walking figures continued to block his route to safety. It was only after some minutes that Adam realised that the dark figures were those of Mary and Catherine, being escorted home by two members of the Barritt family. At last, Adam heard farewells being called, and after the sound of all footsteps had faded into a complete silence, he felt it was safe to regain the road. With a pounding heart, the man covered the last few yards to reach the haven of the stables. His now trembling fingers tore away at the four mud-caked sacks on the legs of his horse, intent on removing all evidence of his skulduggery. With the animal now returned to the hay, Adam left the stables and crossed the yard swiftly, making for the kitchen door. With each step taken, a wave of relief washed over him, and the pounding in his breast began to subside as he advanced towards this safe haven. Reaching the threshold, the door opened before him, and as he passed through he almost fell into the open arms of Mary. The two embraced and kissed violently in an explosion of passion. No words were spoken, nor any sound uttered as they clung to each other for what seemed an eternity. At length, Mary forced her lips away from Adam's. With one hand she pulled at Adam's shoulder, and raising her other hand, held an upright finger to her mouth in a gesture of silence. Guiding her accomplice across the kitchen floor and up the stairs, they passed Catherine's room and into Mary's chamber, pausing only momentarily to close the wooden door. To the now panting man, no further invitation was necessary. In feverish haste he pulled off his boots and loosened his breeches. By the flickering light of the candles stationed on a side chest of drawers, he watched in hot anticipation as Mary cast off her blouse and petticoats. Adam hesitated no longer, and seizing her they fell together on the bed, consummating their love in a frenzy of lust until all passion finally expired. Exhausted, they lay side-by-side. No sounds were audible from the lovers other than the rapid gasps of their breath upon the night air. In time even this slight interruption to the stillness of the night subsided as the couple fell into a deep sleep.

Chapter Four

Strong shafts of light were streaming through the shutters when Adam felt himself roused from a deep slumber. It was Mary lying by his side, gently shaking his shoulder.

'My dearest Adam,' Mary whispered in his ear, and put her arms lovingly around his prone figure. ''Tis done now and all over. But we must be patient and play our parts with guile, then nobody will suspect us.'

Adam quickly recalled the events of the previous day, but as Mary's naked body drew closer to his, he instantly dismissed such thoughts from his mind. Responding to Mary's warm overtures, he engaged instantly, responding to a sudden flush of hot desire. Their lovemaking only ended when they fell apart, exhausted from their exertions.

'I love you,' Mary said softly. 'All will be well, but we must be very careful. Sarah'll be back at noon and we must show all that nothing is amiss. Come, let's dress and take breakfast with Catherine.'

Soon they went downstairs. By the time that Adam had washed the grime from his face and hands at the yard pump, bread, ale and a plate of cold lamb chops were waiting on the kitchen table for him.

For the first time that Mary could ever remember, the two sisters and Adam were sitting down together to eat.

'All is well, Catherine,' Mary said in a reassuring voice. 'Remember to keep your oath and none of us have anything to fear.'

Catherine did not reply. She appeared to be in a daze and mechanically picked at her food, occasionally dropping meat bones to a waiting mongrel stationed at her feet. It was as if she was in a prolonged state of shock, unable to believe what had taken place. The ale tasted bitter to her. She began to cough, and rose from the table. In an agitated state, she fled from the kitchen to the sanctuary of her room. There, as the reality of the situation seized her, she opened her mouth as if to call out for help, but no sound escaped her lips. She tried to pray but was unable. She felt a murderess.

Mary and Adam exchanged worried looks as Catherine left the room.

'You sure she'll not blab?' Adam asked.

'Not to worry my love,' Mary consoled. ''Twill take time for her to settle, but she took the oath well enough and will not tell a soul of what took place.'

Breakfast ended, the couple set about covering up all remaining traces of the previous night's deeds. The eight sacks used to muffle the horses' hooves were consigned to the kitchen fire and reduced to unrecognisable ashes. Small clods of earth carried inadvertently into the house and study on Adam's boots were carefully taken up. Outside, to Adam's dismay, some darkened but unmistakable stains of blood were still visible near to where the vicar had been buried. Taking the spade again, he quickly covered the telltale stains with fresh gravel.

Satisfied that all evidence of the murder had been hidden, the couple met again in the kitchen. It was now late in the morning and Mary realised that she needed to take the food basket out to John Jordan and Will working in the field. It was with no little relief that she was able to leave the heavy atmosphere which now prevailed within the vicarage, and was able to walk with a firm step, carrying her basket of ale, cheese and bread to the two men who were hedging and ditching near the Northfield.

'Is the master at 'ome, mistress?' enquired Jordan, saluting Mary with an almost imperceptible push to his hat with a long finger. 'I'd like a word wi'im about next Sunday's service.'

'Uncle left last night for Patrington,' was the bland reply, 'but I expect him back before noon.'

'Right y'are. I'll be up later,' he said.

Mary turned for home but she did not hurry, her mind fully occupied with thoughts of a very different life ahead. At length she regained sight of the church and the familiar thatched cottages grouped about the grey-stoned and cobbled tower. Suddenly, her attention was diverted to the small figure of a girl running towards her. It was Sarah, returned from her visit home, in great haste, her skirt billowing behind her.

As Sarah approached, Mary felt her heart begin to pound, but she did her utmost to appear calm and assumed a suitable puzzled look to confront the girl.

'Come quickly, Mistress Mary! Come quickly, they've found the master's 'orse. Summat dre'dful's 'appened to Mr Sinclare.'

Mary held the shoulders of the excited girl and feigned a worried expression. 'Go and fetch John Jordan from yonder field. Tell him to come immediately to the vicarage.'

All was well, Mary thought to herself, and she felt a growing confidence as she began to play the part she had rehearsed in her mind so many times in the past few hours.

Sarah ran off on her new errand whilst Mary, now with more hurried steps, continued on towards the vicarage. Even from a distance she could see a group of people had already gathered outside the house. In the midst of the group she recognised the short, rotund figure of Mr John Pighills, the rector of Patrington. Closer now, she could see the cleric talking to three locals, Grimston Cookman, Laurence Barritt and John Jeggar. A few yards from this party, Mary saw Adam and the rector's man, John Turner, holding three horses, one of which was clearly her uncle's chestnut horse.

Grimston Cookman was the first to catch sight of Mary, and he came forward to greet her with a concerned expression on his face.

'Sorry to bring some bad news, mistress,' Cookman began. 'But we're right worried about the Reverend – your uncle, that is.'

'Why, whatever is the matter?' Mary asked.

'Well, it's like this 'ere,' Cookman went on. 'Some men were at work this morning early, near the sea at Holmpton, when they comes across this animal.' He pointed to the vicar's chestnut. 'All saddled up 'an all, but no rider. One of the men took it to Patrington, where Mr Pighills 'ere reckoned it was Mr Sinclare's. True enough, Adam tells us that it is Mr Sinclare's horse, but where is he?'

By this time John Pighills had reached Mary and he extended both his hands to hold hers.

'My dear,' he said with deep concern in his voice. 'I fear your uncle may have met with a misfortune, for I hear he left late last night to visit me.' Mary nodded and allowed the rector to continue. 'He certainly did not reach my house and nobody in the neighbourhood saw him. Is it true he left about nine in the evening? Alone?' Mary nodded again. 'A strange time to set out,' mused the rector. 'The chances are that he has met with a bad fall and let us hope, with God's help, he has already been found and is cared for somewhere.'

'What do you plan to do?' Mary asked.

'My dear, it will be best if we form search parties, and each one covers a different area, combing the fields and ditches. It is very strange indeed that your uncle chose such a late hour to travel alone. And why was his horse at Holmpton, so far from the direct road?'

Mary followed the rector's words intently, and her worried

expression was not wholly one of deception. When the chance allowed, she gave a furtive glance in Adam's direction, but if he was overhearing their conversation it did not show, as he appeared to be fully occupied talking to the rector's man.

''Tis the only thing to be done,' said Mary. 'Adam and John Jordan must join the search. You must leave at once for there is no time to be lost. My poor uncle may well be lying in some lonely place with a broken leg.'

There was a grunt of approval from all around Mary, and as Cookman began to organise search parties, she noticed out of the corner of her eye, a little way off from the men, a group of village women had gathered nearby. The noise of their chatter rose in volume as the numbers increased; the news being retold and embroidered with each new arrival. Mary, who had never been one to mix socially with the village women, and who was, therefore, a frequent subject of their gossiping tongues, stared coldly at the women, and mused that the events of that day would keep their tongues clacking for the rest of their lives.

By this time, most of the men had left to speedily saddle up their horses and begin the search. With the assistance of his man, Mr Pighills was up in the saddle and waved farewell to Mary.

'Does my sister know what has happened?' asked Mary to the mounted man.

'No, my dear. Adam here said she is unwell, so I fear this unhappy task will fall on your shoulders. Pray do not alarm her. With God's help we'll bring your uncle back with no more than a bruise or two. Have his bed warmed, a good fire on and some brandy at the ready!'

With these last instructions, the rector pulled at the brim of his hat and motioned his horse away from the vicarage to join Cookman, who had reappeared about fifty yards distant at the head of a party of riders. The rector was followed by John Turner, and some moments later Adam emerged from the stables, mounted on the vicar's horse. He rode by close to Mary, and with an unconcealed smirk of triumph upon his face, waved to the lone woman. Mary, taken aback at the sight of Adam on her uncle's horse, gave a worried look to her lover.

'Take care Adam,' she called softly as he passed.

'Never fear, my love, there's nowt t'go wrong,' was the confident reply as he rode away to join the others. Seconds later, Jordan cantered out of the stable yard, riding the horse usually taken by Adam. With a wave of his whip he saluted Mary and was soon away up the road. A few cries of encouragement to the riders from the village women sharply reminded Mary of their presence. She inwardly noted that they had remained curiously hushed during the previous few moments, seeing Adam's departure on the vicar's horse.

'My God,' she thought to herself, 'we must have a care.' She turned on her heels and went into the house to meet a wide-eyed Sarah in the kitchen.

'Sarah,' commanded the mistress. 'If there are any callers, I cannot attend them. I shall be with Mistress Catherine.'

The girl bobbed a curtsy of understanding, and watched her mistress climb the stairs and disappear from view. The young girl had never known such goings-on in all her life and drank in the heady drama to the full.

The afternoon sun had lost its power to warm by the time the search parties returned to Owthorne. With the exception of one man, the riders were downhearted and dejected at their lack of success. The area between Hollym, Holmpton and Patrington had been scoured; every field and ditch covered; every cow house inspected, but without revealing the smallest clue concerning the whereabouts of the missing parson. The men talked over the possible causes for the disappearance for the tenth time, and still remained baffled. Cookman sought out Adam in the yard and attempted once again to go over all the events of the previous evening. Rather to his surprise, Cookman found Adam's replies unhelpful and his manner supercilious.

'I tell you, parson was right out o'sorts. Banged about the place. Shouted fer 'is 'oss,' was Adam's only contribution to the enquiry.

Cookman persisted. 'Where did 'ee say 'ee we're going?'

'Patrin'ton.'

''Ad 'ee a gun wi'im?'

'Dunno.'

'Did 'ee say when 'ee'd be back?'

'Nivver sed a word.'

Cookman gave up the verbal struggle, but the servant's callous and detached manner did not go unnoticed. However, at the time, he ascribed it simply to a well-known knowledge of Adam's dislike of his master. Distraction came when Sarah brought out a tray of tankards of ale for the tired men. They drank gratefully but did not stay long, only pledging to continue the search on the next day, which was a Sunday.

John Jordan opened the church door early on Sunday morning. The villagers, too, arrived well before the usual hour for the service, not entering the church, but waiting outside, as if to expect to see at any moment the broad figure of their vicar arrive to lead them into church. Nothing happened to fulfil their hopes, and turned eleven o'clock, Cookman walked over to the vicarage to speak to Mary.

'We'll be on our way again,' he said, ''oping as we shall 'ave more luck this time in finding Mr Sinclare, safe and sound, please God.'

'What will you do if you don't find uncle?' Mary asked cautiously.

'Don't rightly know, mistress. I hadn't thought about that.' Cookman looked puzzled and scratched his forehead.

'At any rate,' he said finally, 'I'm sure we'll find your uncle today, but if needs be, I cud go off to Hedon to tell Mr Waterland we've lost our vicar. But it wouldn't make a lot of sense to any of us. Well, I must be off, mistress.'

'Good luck then,' Mary said in farewell, and watched Cookman as he walked away and out of the yard.

'So we'll have Henry Waterland round here soon enough,' she thought, turning to go back into the vicarage.

That evening a dispirited and exhausted party of men returned to the vicarage and informed of their failure to find their vicar. Mary was surprised to see Samuel Owbridge amongst the party. Owbridge was the local tailor and not a man accustomed to spending a day in the saddle. She mused that his presence in the search party showed how much the villagers were anxious to find their missing vicar.

'Not a 'air of the man to be seen, mistress. I've never known naught like it,' Owbridge said to Mary.

'I'm sure you've all done your very best,' Mary replied, now showing a well-rehearsed air of both sympathy and resignation.

'Don't know what's to be done now, mistress, 'cos we must all get back to work in the morn. Take heart though, Grimston's took off for Hedon to tell Mr Waterland. He'll be back late tonight.'

With nothing more to say, Mary thanked the men again for their trouble and wished them all a good night. The men in their turn bade her goodnight and watched as she walked back into the house. The heavy oak door closed behind her, and she was enveloped by the arms of the waiting Adam, concealed in the shadows of the kitchen. That night Adam forsook his customary rough bed in the stables and slept with Mary in the house. Their love, finally truly consummated, reflected their months of frustration and saw a release of pent-up emotion, with all caution thrown to the wind.

* * * * *

As dawn was breaking, Mary had the good sense to make Adam leave her bedroom. With some show of bad grace, he returned to his loft in the stables before Sarah was up and about. The deep stillness of the world at that hour, broken only by the constant dull noise of the sea and the intermittent cries of the gulls, was no calming balm to the restless man. His intent now was to enjoy all the perquisites of his new situation, and with an ever impatient greed.

Unable to rest further, he strode into the stables, saddled the best horse, mounted with ease and urged the animal out onto the road. With no fixed destination in mind, he galloped away from the village and did not ease up until he reached a small cove on the shoreline near Tunstall. There some boats were moored high and dry on the shingle, for the moment empty and still. For a while Adam was alone, absorbed with his own thoughts as he gazed at the white-crested waves approaching and retreating with unfailing regularity.

In time, the scene was enlivened by the arrival of four men carrying long jute nets over their shoulders. Adam recognised the men as being members of the Handson family, and responded to their greeting with a gruff acknowledgement. He watched the men prepare their nets and launch two boats. Slowly, the boats pulled away from the shore as the fishermen began their steady, rhythmic work at the oars. Adam watched the two boats rise to the horizon and fade from view. For all that had passed in these last few days, his fascination with the sea had not diminished.

Chapter Five

By the time Adam returned to the vicarage, several folk were about their business and watched him turn into the stable yard. He ignored them. Meat and ale awaited him in the house, where he sprawled in what had been the vicar's old seat. He called for Sarah to fetch and carry at his pleasure. The girl was taken aback at this sudden change in Adam's behaviour. Here was a servant whose position in the household, she felt, was somewhat akin to her own, and who was now adopting fancy airs, taking unheard of liberties and giving her orders. She looked to her mistress for guidance. Mary firmly nodded her approval and motioned to Sarah to replenish Adam's tankard, which had been thrust somewhat menacingly in her direction.

'Mr Adam,' said Mary, with a heavy emphasis on the new title, 'is the man of the house now, and his needs should be attended to promptly.'

Sarah heard the words and caught sight of a smile of satisfaction which passed between Mary and Adam. She did not understand. How could a fellow servant suddenly become the master of the house? Why did her mistress entertain and encourage the servant? And above all, where was Mr Sinclare?

Sarah held her tongue and meekly tilted the contents of the pitcher of ale into the proffered tankard. Breakfast over, however, it was not long before the young girl was relating these strange happenings to John Jordan, who had called in at the vicarage with a pail of milk.

'That's a rum 'un, that is,' he said, scratching the bald top of his head. 'A rum 'un if ever there was.' Jordan, never one to keep his thoughts to himself, soon reached Galloway's house, where a gathering quickly assembled, eager to share any crumb of gossip which Jordan had culled from the vicarage.

The next day, good fortune attended the two lovers in the form of the arrival of a breathless Grimston Cookman at the vicarage.

'Sorry, I've only bad tidings, mistress,' he began. 'They've found Mr Sinclare's wig and riding whip near Holmpton. Not far from where they found 'is 'oss.'

Mary's heart raced at the news. The plan seemed to be working perfectly, but she quickly composed herself and put on a concerned air.

'Near Holmpton, you say? Exactly where, pray?'

'They say as half-way down cliff. Looks proper bad, I fear. Mr Sinclare must have gone o'er the edge in the dark.

'That's terrible,' Mary replied. 'I'm afraid it does look as if poor uncle has met with a fearful accident.'

'Right enough,' Cookman agreed. 'We'll 'ave to wait and see what Mr Waterland'll make of the matter. He promised to come o'er 'ere today.'

'Indeed,' Mary said, 'but my thanks to you for coming to tell me about this discovery. I'll await Mr Waterland's arrival in the house.'

Mary saw Cookman out and closed the house door. Inwardly she felt a growing excitement that all would be well. Now that the wig and whip had been found, she had good reason to feel secure. To the outside world, Henock Sinclare had left the vicarage alone late one evening, and then by accident, in the dark, had fallen over the cliff edge. Whatever thoughts the villagers might harbour, Mary felt that no blame could fall on Adam or herself, unless there was a chance discovery of the grave in the yard. The only matter that gave Mary some unease in her rare moments of self-reflection was the behaviour of the only other witness to the crime.

Catherine now spent most of her day alone in her room. In solitude, she took to bouts of weeping, or spent long periods gazing vacantly out of her bedroom window. At meal times, Sarah took a tray up to Catherine's chamber, leaving it outside the sister's door. Often the young girl returned to find the tray untouched, but to the unknowing, this behaviour only seemed to be a sincere sign of grief shown by a niece for her missing uncle.

It was gone two o'clock that day when Henry Waterland reached Owthorne and guided his horse into the yard of the vicarage. Waterland was an imposing figure of a man, in his prime, approaching thirty-five years of age. He had come to Hedon from Lincolnshire and had set up a lawyer's practice in the borough. Eight years ago he had married the daughter of Alderman Baines, and only last year he himself had been made an alderman and elected mayor of the small borough.

Mary came out of the house to greet the visitor. Although she kept her attention fixed on the new arrival, she was acutely aware that a number of villagers had already gathered at the yard gates and were watching events. Waterland held Mary's hands in his and spoke in a low voice.

'I wish I was here in happier circumstances, my dear. Any news of your uncle?'

'I'm afraid not, Mr Waterland,' Mary replied. 'We have nothing but uncle's horse, and I have heard that a wig and whip have been discovered on the cliffs by the seashore at Holmpton.'

'But no sign of the man?'

'Nothing. I fear the sea has claimed poor uncle and he has been swept away.'

At that point the pair were joined in the yard by Grimston Cookman, Laurence Barritt and William Lowry.

'Gentlemen, do come inside.' Mary reached out and gently pulled at Waterland's arm to guide him and the others into the house and away from the stares of the onlookers. 'He seems to have disappeared completely,' she said finally.

'Great heavens above,' exclaimed Waterland. Then turning to the men, he added, 'Whatever is to be done?'

'That, Sir, is what'n we're all 'oping you're going to tell us,' was Cookman's quick retort.

After an intake of breath, the lawyer looked at Mary with an air of resignation.

'I fear the villagers expect me to perform some miracle and produce your uncle from out of thin air. I wish to God 'twere possible, but I hear two careful searches have found nought. It's a complete mystery. A man leaves here last Friday evening and has not been seen since. It seems he may have met with an accident by the cliffs at Holmpton.'

'That's right, Sir,' said Cookman. 'His wig an' whip were found on the cliff edge, altho' why Mr Sinclare would choose such a dangerous path on a dark night has confounded us all.'

'Forgive me, Mr Waterland,' Mary interjected. 'You must be fatigued after your ride. Sarah! Bring ale for Mr Waterland and the other gentlemen.'

Cookman held up his hand in polite refusal, apologising on behalf of the three men, saying that they needed to return to the fields. Waterland, left alone with Mary in the parlour, accepted the drink and seated himself in a comfortable, high-backed chair.

'Damn it,' he began. 'A man cannot just vanish. It isn't natural. I've never heard the like of it. Never.' After a moment's thought, he turned to Mary.

'My dear, with your permission I should like to look over your uncle's study. Who knows? There may be a letter or some writing that can cast light on this affair.'

'Of course,' Mary replied. 'Please feel at liberty to go and do as you wish, anywhere in the house. Our only desire is that our dear uncle returns to us safe and with all speed.'

Mary contrived to adopt a suitable tone in her voice, and met the lawyer's concerned gaze with a look of feigned anguish. Rewarded by a smile of sympathy, Mary led the lawyer to the study.

'I'll leave you to your searchings, Mr Waterland. I must needs go and comfort my sister, who is taking this all most hard.'

'I'm right sorry to hear that,' said Waterland. 'Please give my respects to Miss Catherine. Tell her to be of good heart, for we may yet find your uncle alive and well.'

Alone in the study, Waterland set about his task with a lawyer's trained eye for detail. No item escaped his careful search; no document was left unread. At last, when every drawer in the vicar's bureau had been combed for clues, and every sheet of paper had been scrutinised, the lawyer acknowledged defeat. Bewildered, he left the study, intent on finding Mary. On the way he encountered Sarah, who informed him that Cookman wished to have a word with him outside the vicarage. Hoping that there might be some fresh news of the vicar, Waterland wasted no time in leaving the house. At once he noted a group of men, including Cookman, standing some way off, and although they were aware of his presence, he felt it strange that they made no movement in his direction.

'Good day, all,' said Waterland, at last reaching the men. A low murmur in response to the greeting was cut short by the voice of Cookman.

'Mr Waterland, forgive us calling you out, but there are some strange goings on here, and much ugly talk is beginning to go abroad.'

'Speak up, man,' commanded the lawyer, with a new tone of apprehension.

'Well, sir, it's those things found at Holmpton.'

Laurence Barritt stepped forward, and from a sack produced a limp, sodden and dirty but recognisable wig and a horsewhip.

'You have no doubt they belong to Mr Sinclare?' asked Waterland.

'No doubtin', it's for sure,' Barritt replied.

'Where do you say they were found?'

'Near the beach at Holmpton, caught on the clay at the foot of the cliffs.'

'Then amen to that,' said Waterland. 'I'm afraid to say there's no hope for Mr Sinclare. For some reason he must have taken the cliff path. In the dark, his horse stumbled, throwing the poor man over the cliff to a terrible death.'

'Aye,' replied Cookman. 'That would be an end to the matter all right, but the way we looks on it is different. That's Mr Sinclare's wig and whip; that's right enough, but where's the body?'

'Lying at the bottom of the German Ocean, fathoms deep, I fear.'

'That's as may be,' continued Cookman. 'But Laurence 'ere 'as just come back from the very spot where the wig 'n whip was found. He don't reckon that at this time of the year, full summer, the tide would reach the cliffs.' A general hum of approval supported Cookman's words from all around.

'What are you suggesting?' Waterland asked.

'What we're saying is this'n. Where we found the wig 'n all, we should 'ave found vicar as well. We all believe he's been done to death and 'is body is 'idden in some spot. And there's only one man who could 'ave done it.'

'This is dangerous talk, Cookman,' Waterland interjected in alarm. 'To start talking of foul murder like this will get short shrift from the justices. A wave or two could have reached the cliff and the sea does not always give up its victims.'

'That's not all, Mr Waterland.' Cookman was now determined to administer the coup de grâce to his argument. 'This mornin' John Jordan 'eard a queer tale from Sarah, the young girl at the vicarage. She said that Mary Sinclare forced her to wait on the servant, Adam Alvin, and called him the new man of the house.'

'Sarah's but a child,' interposed Waterland quickly. 'Like as not she didn't understand what her mistress wanted, and at all events, Mistress Mary must be in low spirits now and seeking help where she may.'

'That's all well and good, Mr Waterland. But with respect, sir, we'd like you to question Alvin, to try and find out what really 'appened last Friday night. When Mr Sinclare left us, 'e went to see Alvin there, so 'e must 'ave some story to tell. 'e won't tell us, but you can get it out of 'im.'

The surrounding hum of approval grew louder and left

Waterland with little choice in the matter. He merely gave a curt nod of assent, turned on his heels and walked back into the vicarage. From the moment of his arrival at the village he had felt uncomfortable with this seemingly unsolvable task that had been forced upon him. Now with this latest turn of events the business was becoming sinister.

Sarah opened the front door to admit the lawyer and Mary, who had been watching the scene in the roadway from an upstairs window, quickly descended the stairs.

'Mary, I'll have a few words with Alvin, if you please. From all accounts, he may have been the last person to see your uncle last Friday.'

'I'll call him this instant,' Mary replied.

Adam was soon found, sprawled out on a seat by the kitchen fire. To Mary's dismay she saw a tankard of ale in her lover's hand, and from all appearances it would seem that he had been drinking steadily since breakfast.

'Adam, Mr Waterland wants to talk to you in the study.'

What's 'e want?'

'For God's sake,' said Mary, now in some alarm. 'Be sharp, Adam, or we'll be undone. Mr Waterland is a clever man, so have a care. Watch your tongue and say little. Remember the story – nothing else, mind, and we'll see it through.'

With a heavy sigh, Adam struggled to his feet, steadied himself with one hand on the kitchen table, and with a mumbled curse, lurched off in the direction of the study.

Waterland had never cared much for Henock Sinclare's servant, a surly lad who never showed the slightest gratitude for all that the vicar had done to improve his lot in life. Waterland had already surmised that of all the villagers in Owthorne, the servant would be the least concerned about his master's disappearance. Waterland, however, was quite unprepared to interview a near drunken man, and as Adam swayed slowly from side to side on the threshold of the study, it took him a few moments to appreciate the situation. The silence was finally broken by Adam.

'Mary tells me you wants to see me, so 'ere I am.'

'Mistress Mary,' replied the lawyer coldly, with a heavy emphasis on the respectful title, 'passed on my order. Come in. I want to put to you a few questions.'

Adam entered, his eyes roaming about the room for a convenient chair. Waterland ignored the unspoken demand and began his cross-examination.

'Alvin, I understand you may have been the last person to see Mr Sinclare on Friday evening.' A pause produced no verbal reaction from the servant, causing Waterland to continue. 'What was Mr Sinclare wearing when he left?'

'Jus' 'is usual.'

'A hat, for instance?' persisted the lawyer.

'Parsons all'us wears a 'at.'

'Quite so.' Waterland sighed inwardly. 'But Mr Sinclare must have several hats. What colour was it?'

''e only 'ad black uns.'

Waterland admitted defeat on this line of questioning and stared with distaste at the morose figure standing before him. 'Do you remember if Mr Sinclare carried a whip when he left?'

'Don't you take yorn when yer goes out?'

'I'm putting the questions,' flashed back the lawyer, 'and I'll trouble you to keep a civil tongue in your head and remember your place. I'm warning you, your manner and feelings for your master are well-known to me and to all decent folk hereabouts. When Mr Sinclare returns, the first thing I'll recommend is that he'll bring you to account for your behaviour today.'

Adam, steadied by this unexpected rebuke, approached Waterland. An unmistakable smirk of triumph appeared on his face. 'Mr Sinclare won't never return to punish me.'

The lawyer stared at the servant in surprise. 'Pray tell me why?' Waterland waited for Adam to reply, but only received a look of haughty disdain from the servant. Waterland tried again. 'Not come back. Not come back. Why is that?'

''Cos 'e left 'ere of a Friday night for Patrin'ton. They've found 'is 'oss and now as I 'eard it, they brought up parson's wig 'n whip from the sands. The 'ole village is blabbing about it.'

Adam's look of arrogance cut the lawyer to the heart, but he remained silent as Adam continued with his version of events. 'Parson's gone o'er the edge, that's all. 'e'll not come back. Now it's my turn to give orders about this place an' there's a fair deal to put right an' 'all.'

Waterland sprang to his feet, his patience exhausted and unable to control his anger. 'Damn your orders, man!' he cried. 'Your place is in the stables and that's where you'll stay, Mr Sinclare being here or no.'

'You're wrong again, Mr Waterland.'

Waterland allowed the luxury of heavy sarcasm in his voice. 'Is that so? Then pray tell me why?'

''Cos I'm going to marry Mistress Mary, that's why, Mister Waterland.'

Stopped dead in his tracks, the lawyer's eyes opened wide in astonishment. Bewildered and speechless, he floundered in amazement as the broad smirk of triumph spread fully over Adam's face. At length Waterland composed himself.

'Very well, Alvin,' he said. 'I shall speak presently with your mistress, but I warn you, take a care! Don't overstep the mark. You can go now.'

Adam gave a final insolent shrug of his shoulders and left the study and a very distracted Henry Waterland, still in shock from what he had just heard. Alone in the study, the lawyer went over the facts of the case as he knew them. He could not escape the conclusion that the vicar was probably dead, either by accident or by foul play. The villagers clearly wanted to pin a crime on Alvin, an arrogant, insufferable man disliked by all, but where was the victim? No body, no trial, he thought, and then he thought again of possible motives for the servant to want to kill his master. This appeared to be evident, for if Alvin did indeed marry Mary Sinclare, he stood to gain much from the vicar's estate through his wife. If this were all true, Waterland mused, had he been a lone agent? Waterland could not bring himself to believe that Mary would have been a party to such a terrible crime.

'This will never do,' he said to himself, pulling his body out of the study chair and making for the half-open door. He had not gone far when he found Mary waiting in the hall.

'Mary, I'd like a word with you in the study, if you please.' He allowed Mary to pass by and followed her into the room. 'I've had a most unpleasant interview with Alvin.' Mary remained silent. 'He stated to me that he intends to marry you. Is this true?'

'Upon my word,' Mary replied. 'I didn't want the news to be abroad so soon, but I see Adam's told you, so let it be.'

'For the Lord's sake, Mary, I'm not one to preach, and it's not a question of Alvin being a servant, but your uncle would never have consented to such a match. Here we are trying to trace your poor uncle, when in the midst of our troubles, you plan to wed the very man many around here think had some part in your uncle's disappearance.

It just will not do.'

Mary raised her eyes to meet Waterland's stare, and now, more than ever, her determination and strong will came to the fore as she faced the lawyer.

'I care not for the malicious, wagging tongues of the folk here,' she said. ''Tis well known that my uncle was against our marriage, but his reasons were selfish ones. My sister and I have been nought but servants like Adam these past years. My uncle allowed no will to prevail here but his own, and if this affair had not come to pass, we should have run away together.'

'We know about Mr Sinclare's wig and whip being found . . .'

'Yes,' Mary interrupted the lawyer, keeping an even tone to her voice. 'I think that settles the matter.'

'It does and it does not,' replied Waterland, deliberately slowing the pace of his words to give heightened emphasis. 'If the tide washed them in, it should also have returned your uncle's body. I speak plainly, Mary. The whole village believes your uncle has been murdered and Alvin is a suspect.'

'Let them talk with their vipers' tongues,' replied the woman with a flash of anger. 'None hereabout like or understand Adam. The devil take the lot of 'em!'

'Mary, as a family friend, please take my advice. Don't marry Alvin, or if you insist, don't wed here in this parish, or I'll not answer for the consequences.'

'I'm not afraid of the village gossips, Mr Waterland. Be assured we shall not be deterred from our plans. We care not for that miserable crew outside.'

Waterland found his hat and whip on a small table in the parlour and made for the door. He paused at the threshold and, turning to Mary, he made a parting declaration.

'Sadly, I see you are determined on this unwise course. I can say no more than before. I now believe that your uncle has met with an untimely death, God rest his soul. This being so, it remains my duty to look to the spiritual needs of the parishioners – that "miserable crew" as you call them. I shall send Mr Prowde, the curate at Hedon, to come and minister at St Peter's until such time as a new incumbent is appointed to the living. Good day, Miss Mary.'

Waterland gave a curt bow to the woman and quickly left the house to look for his horse in the stables.

Grimston Cookman and a few other farmers were still gathered a short distance from the vicarage when Waterland emerged riding his horse. All eyes looked up to the lawyer, eager to glean the latest information. To the disappointment of all, however, their curiosity was not to be satisfied. Waterland merely explained that he intended to send a curate from Hedon to take Sunday services until the mystery of Mr Sinclare's disappearance had been solved.

'But what about Adam Alvin?' Cookman demanded in a truculent manner. 'What's to be done wi'im?'

'Nothing,' replied Wateland. 'You know as well as I do, nothing can be proved against him. Nothing at all. You must find Mr Sinclare. Like all of you, I fear he has expired in some way, God rest his soul, but I urge you to continue searching the beach, and indeed the whole area, to put an end to this mystery.'

Without more ado, Waterland bade farewell to the men and rode off at a smart pace in the direction of Patrington. A silent crowd of bystanders watched him depart, and heard the dull thumping of the horse's hooves on the hard clay surface of the road become fainter as the figure of the lawyer receded into the distance. The silence was broken by John Jordan.

'No sense in standing about 'ere all day,' he said. 'There's werck to be done and we must do it. I expect Mr Waterland will see t' matters now.' Then catching the eye of Will Fallowdown, he gave a command. 'Come on lad, let's be off.'

There was a general murmur of agreement from all the men around Jordan, and each departed from the scene, followed by a few of the village women who had gathered nearby hoping to glean some titbits of gossip from the situation.

Chapter Six

On his return to The Hall at Hedon, Henry Waterland wasted no time in setting about the business of the Owthorne vicarage. After describing to his shocked wife, Mary, the events surrounding the disappearance of Mr Sinclare, Waterland sat down to write a letter to David Sinclare, a farmer at Kilham. As far as Waterland was aware, this man was the sole surviving half-brother of Henock Sinclare and his legal next-of-kin. In the letter Waterland related all he knew of the circumstances surrounding the case, and did not fail to write, albeit without comment, about the strange situation which had arisen concerning the attachment of the vicar's niece to the manservant Adam Alvin. Finally, he urged Sinclare to visit Owthorne as soon as possible. This task completed, Waterland carefully sanded his writing, folded the paper, and having lit a candle, secured the folds with hot wax and made a firm impression with his personal seal. Calling for his clerk, Sam Wright, he bade the young man take the letter to Kilham without delay.

By the time Wright emerged from the stables astride his nag, Waterland was already making his way along the cobbled streets of Hedon, intent on finding the Borough's vicar, the Reverend Richard Sissison. The Hedon vicarage belied its imposing-sounding name. It was, in fact, a mean, half-timbered thatched cottage standing next to a row of widows' almshouses in Souttergate. The vicar did not reside there, but in far more elegant surroundings at Burstwick. The small cottage at Hedon served as the home of Samuel Prowde, Mr Sissison's impoverished curate.

Fortune smiled on Waterland that afternoon, as he found the two clerics talking together in the street, this venue obviously being quieter and more commodious than inside the house, which was permanently overrun by Mr Prowde's numerous children.

'Good day, Reverends.' Waterland greeted the men, touching the broad upturned brim of his hat.

'Good day indeed , sir, an unexpected pleasure to be sure,' Sissison effused in reply.

'Sadly, gentlemen, I have brought some unhappy news. Our good friend, Mr Sinclare at Owthorne, has vanished and cannot be found. All the signs indicate that he has met with a most tragic accident.'

Waterland then continued to tell the two men all that had

happened during his visit to Owthorne.

'Dear me, dear me!' the vicar exclaimed at last. 'You really think the poor man is dead?'

'I fear the worst,' answered the lawyer. 'For that reason I have come to you now, as we have a church and a parish with no spiritual guidance.'

'Dear me!' repeated Sissison. 'We must act at once to provide a cure for the souls in that unfortunate parish.'

'Quite so.' Waterland nodded in agreement. 'What do you have in mind?'

'I feel sure I can encompass Owthorne myself. It is but a short ride there from my residence at Burstwick, and Samuel here can help out whenever necessary.'

'But sir,' Waterland rejoined. 'You have Preston also under your wing. Can another parish be added to your burden?'

'Indeed, sir, an added burden to be sure, but we must do the work of the Lord when called upon, and without complaint. Samuel here can take the services on the Lord's Days until his Grace gives me proper authority to serve the parish. I should be much obliged, Mr Waterland, if you would write to Bishopthorpe on my behalf. The living is, of course, held by the Crown, but a word from you to his Grace will smooth the way mightily to the satisfaction of all.'

Waterland had long deprecated the desire of many clergy who sought to collect valuable benefices, but he quickly realised that in the circumstances thrust upon him, the proposal offered by the Reverend was a speedy and convenient solution to the problem.

'I'll see to it immediately,' Waterland replied. 'Please be aware that I've sent word to Kilham, where Mr Sinclare's half-brother resides. I expect to hear from him in a matter of days.' The lawyer again touched the brim of his hat, and after acknowledging similar salutes from the two clerics, he turned away and retraced his steps back to The Hall.

* * * * *

David Sinclare was some years older than his half-brother, Henock. Named after his father and being the only son from his father's first marriage, he had inherited the family farm at Kilham. Now a widower, he had outlived five of his eight children. The Sinclare name still endured, however, with the survival into adulthood of his last-born child, Enock, named after his clerical uncle at Owthorne.

After reading the contents of Henry Waterland's letter, David called for his daughter Anne. She was his eldest surviving child, now in her late thirties and the one who kept house for the family at Kilham.

'Dammit!' David exploded. 'There's some rum goings on down at Owthorne.'

Anne looked quizzically at her father, but said nothing and waited for him to say more.

'Your uncle Henock's gone missing,' David continued. 'They reckon he's met with an accident somewhere, but they can't find him. Things look bad and they fear the worst.'

'I'm right sorry to hear that, father. But what will you do?'

'That's not all,' David interjected. 'Your cousin Mary is going to marry Adam Alvin, that boy Henock brought up after that shipwreck years ago.'

'Never!' cried Anne in surprise. 'What's she want to do that for? He's only a servant, isn't he? I've never taken to him myself, him and his dowly ways.'

David shrugged his shoulders. 'Upon my soul,' he said, 'it's all very queer, but I must go to Owthorne to find out what's what. Henry Waterland's saying the sooner the better, so, my love, can you pack me a bag, sharpish? I'll see Enock afore I go and tell him what's to be done on the farm.'

An hour later, armed with a few spare clothes packed into a linen bag, David Sinclare wasted no time in taking to the road, riding post haste to Owthorne. On the journey David was forced to admit to himself that he had rarely visited his half-brother at the seaside vicarage. In truth, years ago David had harboured feelings of jealousy at Henock's obvious intellectual superiority – never more so than when Henock had left the village to study at Cambridge. From that moment on Henock had been destined for the cloth, whilst David would remain solidly at the plough, following the family tradition at Kilham. All this, however, was well in the past, and for David, years of successful husbandry had proved to be a powerful remedy against all his former feelings of inferiority.

In his desire for speed, the rider took the direct route, albeit winding, through the villages of Burton Agnes, Lissett and Ulrome. He then followed an earth track southwards on to the village of Atwick, thereafter keeping the German Ocean close on his left-hand side.

He maintained a good speed, and reached the Market Place at Hornsea in a little under two hours. His stay at the Hare and Hounds inn was no more than some thirty minutes, ample time in which to see his horse watered, fed and stabled and to hire a second horse from the landlord. Refusing an invitation to dine, he downed a tankard of ale, settled his account, and set out on the second leg of his journey. He soon discovered that his new mount was a far cry from his own well-cared for mare. The hired nag was slow-footed and markedly reluctant to accommodate David Sinclare's desire for speed. He urged the horse on as best he could, but the villages of Aldbrough, Garton, Hilston and Tunstall came and went in slow procession. At last he saw in the distance wisps of smoke from the chimneys of the huddled cottages at Owthorne, and a few minutes later he reached the gates of the vicarage.

David Sinclare's appearance at Owthorne had been expected, although the occupants of the vicarage had no notion as to what time or even what day he would arrive in their midst. On that particular day, as the evening shadows lengthened, there was no expectation of his arrival, especially at such a late hour.

Mary had spent most of that day searching through her uncle's study. Her quest had been to find the vicar's will, but in this her efforts were thwarted. Not once, but three times, she had carefully combed through all the bonds and papers crammed into the narrow drawers of the vicar's old bureau, but to no avail. She had even taken out all the dusty tomes from the library shelves, but still could find no will. Exasperated, she began to ponder on the matter. Perhaps there was such a document deposited with Henry Waterland at Hedon? She did not know, but with her usual shrewd sense of caution she realised that it would be foolhardy to press the matter at this time with the lawyer at Hedon.

David Sinclare's arrival caught those in the house by surprise, but seeing his mounted figure in the yard, Mary quickly gathered her skirts about her and sallied out to greet her kinsman. A surly Adam followed her out of doors, having been brusquely told by Mary to take her uncle's horse and have it stabled for the night.

'Welcome, uncle,' Mary said. 'It's good to see you, but we hadn't expected your coming so late in the day. Adam will take your horse and see to its needs.'

'Came as soon as I got word from Waterland,' David replied, as he dismounted and passed the reins over to Adam with a curt nod of acceptance.

'But what news of Henock? Have we found him?'

'I'm afraid not,' Mary replied, adopting a suitable air of melancholy. 'We are now quite sure that we'll never see poor uncle again.'

'How so?' David asked, giving his niece a kiss of greeting. 'Mustn't give up so easily. Dammit, a man cannot just vanish into thin air!'

'Indeed, uncle. But all searches have been done with great care.'

Mary went on to recount to her uncle the details of finding the rider-less horse, the whip, wig, and all the fruitless efforts of the search parties.

'I'll not rest 'til I'm satisfied we've left no stone unturned, and I can say our duty to Henock has been proper done.'

'Just so, uncle,' Mary said, wondering what her uncle had in mind. But at that point she thought it best to divert the conversation to safer matters.

'Do come inside, uncle. You must needs rest from your journey.'

Mary led the visitor into the house, where he greeted the waiting Catherine. Although it had been some time since he had seen his young niece, David was shocked to see the pallid face and air of general listlessness about the girl. Under the circumstances, he attributed this to a natural state of anxiety, but had no opportunity to dwell on the matter of Catherine's health, as she stayed in the kitchen preparing supper whilst Mary took him into the parlour.

'I'm afraid we can only put you up in uncle Henock's room, David. We are without help in the house these days, as Sarah, our young girl, has been taken away from us just when we're in most need, so we're obliged to fend for ourselves. But we shall give the mattress a good shaking and find some clean linen to make you comfortable.'

'That would be very obliging,' David rejoined. 'I don't want to be a burden, and in any case, I'm not a man for silken sheets and warming pans.' He forced a laugh, in an attempt to lift the heavy weight of gloom which prevailed throughout the house.

As David Sinclare was aware of Mary's attachment to Adam from Waterland's letter, he was not surprised to see Adam join them for supper.

'No business o' mine what the young folks do,' he thought to himself, and made no comment as they all took their places at the oak table. However, whilst he was prepared to sup with Adam, he was not prepared to be confronted by the servant's manner and attitude, which was morose and truculent. David was not to know that Adam's ill-humour was due to Mary's insistence that he should return to sleep in his old cot above the stables for the duration of her uncle's visit.

Adam's dislike for the unwelcome visitor soon became apparent. 'You 'ere to settle up vicar's accounts?' he demanded, adopting an aggressive air.

'I'm here to find my brother. That's the top and bottom of it,' David retorted coolly, sensing the man's hostility.

Adam ignored the retort, and failing to see Mary's worried glance, continued on the attack.

'Vicar owes me six pounds and I needs 'ave the money quick as yer like, an' being 'is nearest, I expect as you'll be wanting to settle with me.'

'Lord save us!' David exploded. 'You all talk as though my brother is dead. What's been done to find him? Where are the search parties now?'

Fearing that more words from Adam would only antagonise her uncle, Mary quickly interrupted in an attempt to diffuse the situation. 'Uncle, I fear we have all given up hope. Days have passed since uncle Henock left us for Patrington. I must say, the search parties have made thorough enquiries, but to no avail. We believe dear uncle met with a terrible and fatal accident at the cliffs below Holmpton. Surely it is pointless to do more?'

'I'll not give up so easily,' David replied, but he said no more and ate silently, clearly deep in thought.

Silence prevailed throughout the rest of the meal. At the end, Mary was relieved to hear Catherine beg to be excused and to retire to her room. Adam, too, departed, offering mumbled words about needing to see to a horse, leaving Mary alone with the visitor. Once they were settled in comfortable chairs in front of the fire, she cautiously opened up the conversation.

'What do you wish to do in the morning?' she asked.

David leant across to a rack by the side of the fireplace and drew out a clay pipe. He did not reply immediately to Mary's question, but slowly filled the pipe with tobacco from a worn leather pouch taken from his pocket. Mary proffered a lighted spill from the fire, and allowed David to draw in several times before he spoke.

'I'll organise a party early in the morning, and we'll search every nook and cranny. One way or another, we must find Henock.'

'As you please, David.' Mary adopted a meek attitude, and only added, 'I suggest you have a word with Jordan, who looks after our farm, in the morning.'

David nodded his head. 'Aye, I need some good folk what knows their way around this part of Holderness. Like as this Jordan'll get me some hard riders for the day.'

Mary was relieved to see that her uncle did not wish to linger around the fire. After the pair had exchanged a few pleasant family memories, and David had smoked his pipe, he rose from the chair.

'By your leave, Mary, I'll take my rest. I'm tired from the journey, and I must be in good fettle for a long day on the morrow.'

'Of course, uncle,' Mary replied. 'I'll get you a candle and see you to your room. I'll bring some hot water up to you at six, rest assured.'

'Thank you kindly, Mary. By hook or by crook I intend to find our Henock and put an end to all this nonsense. Six sharp it is then!'

* * * * *

True to his word, David Sinclare was up and about early the next morning. He found Jordan and Will Fallowdown busy with the cows in Coleman's barn. Straight to the point, he made his needs known, but found Jordan reluctant to go out again on a search for the missing vicar.

'We'n done all that,' Jordan said. 'An' done it all again. It's no use, but I'll tell you, there's a lot of talk around 'ere about what's happened to parson, and many of us don't think he's gone o'er cliff as he's supposed to 'a done.'

David brushed aside the clear implication of Jordan's words. 'We must find my brother,' he maintained. 'I need three or four good riders who'll accompany me on a thorough going over between here and Patrington.'

'It's a proper bad time of the year to be off'n the land,' Jordan rejoined truculently. 'Now's busy days and time lost fills no bellies around 'ere.'

David instantly recognised the un-stated meaning of the Holderness man's words. Raising both his hands to shoulder height in a clear gesture of understanding, he made a final attempt to overcome Jordan's reluctance in the matter. 'All right,' he said. 'Find me three good horsemen by eight o'clock on the morrow, and I'll pay ten shillings a man for a full day's search.'

'Right y'are, gaffer,' Jordan replied, putting aside his previous objections with some alacrity on hearing of the offered reward.

'They'll be ready outside the vicarage at eight sharp.'

Jordan left the barn at a brisk pace, leaving Will to the chore of milking, and David with the distinct feeling that in his anxiety to obtain local help, he had offered too much for what was hardly a full day's work.

It would be needless repetition to describe in detail the events of the next day's search carried out by David and his three hired men. They covered the same ground as the previous search parties had done, riding between Owthorne and Patrington. The beaches, the cliffs, every narrow track and hedge bottom were combed thoroughly; every man and woman seen working in the fields was hailed and questioned, but none could shed any light on the missing man.

By late afternoon the men felt total dismay at their lack of success, and it was inevitable that David's thoughts turned to giving some credence to the dark hints of foul play which the men about him freely offered. At around seven in the evening, he paid off the three men and returned to the vicarage. Mary met the dispirited rider in the yard and held out a tankard of ale, which was gratefully received by the tired man.

'Come inside and take your boots off,' Mary said kindly. 'There's some cold cuts ready for supper.'

Welcome though the food was to David, the general air of gloom which prevailed in the house, coupled with his own feelings of despondency, contributed to long periods of silence around the table. Eventually it was Adam who broke the silence.

'We told yer so, but you wouldn't 'ave it. No doubtin' at all that parson's gone o'er the cliff an' we'll not see 'im again. Now, can I 'ave the six pounds that he was owin' me?'

Mary's eyes shot a worried glance in Adam's direction. She knew full well of her lover's fiery temper and prayed silently that there would be no altercation between Adam and her uncle.

David ignored Adam's demand for money, but faced up to the

servant boldly.

'There's strong talk amongst the men I've been with that my brother may not have met with an accident. Do you know of anyone who would want to cause him harm?'

'You don't want to be listening to all that idle gossip from a cartload of ignorant people 'ereabouts,' Adam cried sharply, before Mary could give an answer to the question. 'They're a fanciful crowd of no-gooders with nothing better to do than spread lies and slanders.'

'Quite so,' Mary interjected quickly. 'They've found uncle's wig and whip near the cliffs and his horse nearby. What more can be said?'

'I suppose not,' said David with a sigh. 'I'll be needing to get back to Kilham in the morning, but I'd better send word to Henry Waterland to ask what's to be done. Without finding Henock it'll make for a rum carry-on, to be sure. In any case, if Henock's dead, they'll want a new parson and he'll want this house. Have you thought what you and Catherine might do?'

Mary thought for a moment before answering her uncle's question. She knew it would be safer to deflect attention away from her attachment to Adam. 'Yes, we've given it some thought,' she said. 'We may go over to stay with friends at Patrington until we find somewhere suitable to live.'

David nodded. 'I'm sure we can find a place for you all at Kilham until things settle down.'

'Thank you most kindly, uncle,' Mary replied. 'But we're comfortable here for the time being. I expect Mr Waterland will arrange for an inventory to be made of all our uncle's chattels.'

'I expect so,' David replied with an air of resignation. 'But be mindful, if I can be of any service whatsoever, I'm nobbut a short ride away.'

David Sinclare's departure from the vicarage early on the following day was something of a relief to Mary. In truth, she had no firm plans for the future, except that she wanted to marry Adam with all possible speed. Quite how this was to be achieved she was unsure. What was certain was that there now existed a deep suspicion all about them of foul play regarding her uncle, and this was patently directed at the man she loved.

Chapter Seven

The Reverend Mr Samuel Prowde, curate of St Augustine's church, Hedon, was a man well accustomed to performing the lion's share of parish work in return for a mouse's reward. Even so, the journey to Owthorne that July Sunday to take the morning service proved to be a welcome diversion from his usual, onerous duties at Hedon and Preston. As his horse jogged along the winding road passing through the villages of South Holderness, his thoughts were directed more on the temporal aspects of his visit to Owthorne, rather than on spiritual ones. The curious disappearance of the vicar there, under such mysterious circumstances, was a matter unique in his experience. He pondered whether or not he should refer to the matter from the pulpit. Some expressions of hope, perhaps? Unfortunately, all that could come to mind in the saddle was the passage including the words, 'in sure and certain hope of the Resurrection . . . ,' from the burial service, which he dismissed as inappropriate for the occasion. Prowde felt annoyed with himself that he had not taken the time to prepare a suitable and truly fitting sermon for the occasion the previous night. Safer, he thought, in view of the season, to rely on the theme of God's goodness and the prospects of a bountiful harvest for all God-fearing men, both to come now on earth and later in Heaven.

Catherine escorted Prowde into the vestry of St Peter's, where John Jordan was waiting to greet the curate. Prowde surmised that the small room, adjoining the chancel, must have remained exactly as Henock Sinclare had left it after taking his last service at the church. Catherine had thoughtfully provided a ewer of warm water, a bowl and towel for the visitor to use to remove the dust of the journey from his face and hands. Jordan rang the church bells, and at eleven o'clock precisely the churchwarden led out the now-robed curate to begin the familiar service of the Lord's day.

The church was crammed, with every box pew occupied. The centre of attention were the three figures seated at the front in the Sinclare box. Sadly, if the good residents of Owthorne, Waxholme and Rimswell, not to mention a few curious, gawping visitors from Withernsea, held out any hope of hearing revelations concerning the missing vicar, they were doomed to disappointment. Prowde maintained a prudent policy of delivering a safe and bland homily, to the utter dissatisfaction of almost all present.

At the end of the service the congregation filed slowly past the curate at the south door. Each gave a somewhat surly mark of farewell; the men touching their hats, and the women acknowledging a slight bow of the head from Prowde with a faint smile of recognition. Mary and Catherine escorted Prowde into the vicarage, where some victuals had been laid out on the kitchen table. As was usual, Catherine made her excuses to the visitor and left the kitchen for her room. Alone with Mary and Adam, Prowde was soon made aware of the matter uppermost on the minds of the couple.

'Mr Prowde,' Mary began, 'Adam and I are intent on marrying without delay. To wed at St Peter's would not be wise, as there are many here showing an ill-will to our union.'

'Why so?' asked the curate, with some degree of false naïveté.

'There are foolish people 'ere,' Adam said. 'They're saying parson didn't fall o'er cliff, and they trump up fanciful ideas that some foul deed 'as been done.'

'In truth,' Mary added, 'it is well-known in the village that my uncle did not approve of our match. We only wish to be married as quickly and as quietly as possible.'

'I see,' said the curate. 'In that case, the only way to avoid having the banns read out in church is to obtain a licence. This needs the approval of my vicar, Mr Sissison at Hedon. May I suggest you go and see my friend Dr Fiddes at Halsham. I'm sure he will be of assistance in this delicate matter, and I'll lay the business of a licence with Mr Sissison on my return to Hedon. By next Sunday, when I come again, I trust we can put your worries to rest.'

Mary and Adam exchanged warm glances of relief and joy.

'That is truly very kind of you,' Mary said. 'We are most grateful. Rest assured, we'll set out for Halsham tomorrow and see what can be arranged with Dr Fiddes.'

* * * * *

The dull warmth of the early morning sun embraced the two riders as they left the vicarage. They ignored the sullen stares of a few neighbours who were standing outside their cottages, whilst a few, better-known to Mary, muttered muted greetings. Soon the cottages were left behind, and Mary and Adam turned their horses into the Hull road, which led to Halsham. For the couple intent in pursuing their desire to marry, it seemed to take them only a short time to reach their destination. Ahead they saw the church and schoolhouse at the side of the road. Turning down a narrow path leading to the church, the couple, riding in single file, made for a nearby cottage close by the chancel. This was the modest, not to say mean, residence of the rector, the Reverend Dr Richard Fiddes.

Mary and Adam were greeted at the front the cottage by the rector himself, who called loudly to his son, Dick, to take the horses from the visitors to a stall at the rear of the house.

With a cheery wave of the arm the rector hailed the visitors.

'Good day, good people. Do come inside the parlour.' Then, catching sight of his wife in the doorway, 'Jane my love, bring a jug of ale, if you please, to slake the thirst of our visitors.'

Jane Fiddes immediately recognised Mary and Adam. The disappearance of Henock Sinclare and the rumours attending the case had spread as fire in a dry hayrick throughout all that part of Holderness, leaving Jane consumed with curiosity as to the purpose of this visit. Nevertheless, she greeted the visitors civilly, withdrew, and after a short interval, re-appeared with tankards and a jug of her small beer. Withdrawing a second time, she discreetly took up a position out of sight by the kitchen door, where she hoped she would be able to overhear what was about to be said.

Dr Fiddes began by expressing to Mary his deep concern over the disappearance of her uncle, and hoped that some happy discovery would soon be made.

'I fear not, Dr Fiddes,' Mary replied solemnly. 'My uncle has surely met with a terrible accident whilst out riding, and we have quite given up all hope.'

'Alas,' replied the rector, with a sigh of resignation. 'It seems so, God rest his soul, amen. But my dear, why has my humble home been chosen today for a visit?'

'Dr Fiddes,' Mary began, 'I'm sure you've heard all the wicked rumours that have been abroad about why my uncle did not return home. They are being spread about by many who have nothing better to do than speak ill of folk who never did them any harm.'

Dr Fiddes nodded imperceptibly. 'I had heard of some such wild talk on the matter,' he murmured.

'Adam and I wish to marry as soon as we may. But we fear that to wed at St Peter's would not be seemly. We've come to ask if you would marry us here at Halsham.'

'Goodness me!' exclaimed the rector. 'I had not imagined

such a thing and at such a time.'

'Our minds are quite made up, Dr Fiddes. Can it be done secretly?'

'I fear not,' said the rector. 'We can avoid the usual banns being published, but we'd need a licence.'

'Is that from Mr Sissison?' Adam interjected.

'Indeed,' replied the rector. 'He is the Archbishop's surrogate and can provide a licence – for a small fee, of course,' he added, with a smile.

'Ah!' Mary exclaimed. 'He is well aware of our plight, as Mr Prowde at Hedon has promised to speak to him on the matter.'

'Can 'e stop us gettin' wed?' Adam asked.

'No, indeed not,' answered the rector. 'If you are resolved to wed, I see no impediment whatsoever to your union. For a fee of half-a-crown I can arrange a quiet nuptial here, but it may take a few days for the licence to be safely in our hands.'

Mary lost no time in opening her purse which was tied around her girdle. The silver coins were passed over to the rector, who slipped them almost imperceptibly into his waistcoat pocket with the deft ease and smooth movement of a man of the cloth about his customary duties.

'My dear, thank you kindly. As soon as I have Mr Sissison's licence to hand, I'll send word with my son Dick, and we can marry you here at Halsham, with God's full blessing.'

Their mission accomplished, Mary and Adam stayed only a short time more to exchange pleasantries. The ride back to Owthorne was uneventful, and the couple returned to the vicarage in high spirits.

The following Sunday the reappearance of Mr Prowde did not, however, advance their plans for matrimony as they had hoped. Mr Sissison was away in London, and the curate had been unable to broach their request for a licence. Adam cursed the absence of Mr Sissison, the inability of Mr Prowde to produce the desired document, and everyone else in general for hindering their plans. To the couple, each day that passed was akin to a month, causing the occupants of the vicarage to feel imprisoned in their home. To divert their growing anxieties concerning the delay, Mary busied herself about the house and saw to the daily needs of Jordan and Will Fallowdown. Adam spent most of his time exercising and grooming the horses, whilst Catherine made secretive excursions at odd times to find comfort in the company of Widow Preston. At the widow's cottage shop the events of recent weeks were never mentioned, and the counsel of the old lady was confined to the state of Catherine's ailments, and suggested remedies to relieve the girl's newly-developed signs of deep melancholy.

* * * * *

David Sinclare had not been idle since his return to Kilham. Although he had been advised by Henry Waterland that at this early stage his half-brother could not be legally declared dead, David was impatient to have matters resolved, and set about to organise some freeholders from Owthorne to carry out the post mortem inventory of the goods and chattels of his half-brother.

On the appointed day, Mary let in the familiar figures of Robert Thompson, Walter Westerdale, Richard Langthorp and John Matchen, over the threshold of the vicarage.

'Beggin' your pardon, Miss Mary,' Thompson began, doffing his hat in Mary's direction. 'We'll be as quick as we can be and not make a fuss.'

'Let me know if I can be of any help,' Mary replied, standing back to let the men enter. 'I think you well know the house and what belonged to my poor uncle.'

'That's right enough, Miss Mary. Dick, John and m'sen 'll do the callin' and Walter 'ere 'll do the scribin'. It won't tak long then we'll 'ave to do the stables and the land.'

'Of course, gentlemen. I understand. Outside, Adam will be at your service if you need help. Pray begin your business.'

All the four men were well versed in carrying out their sombre task, and they set to, carefully listing all the goods that had once belonged to the vicar. Although not a word was said between them within the walls of the house, they were amazed to discover that a man of the vicar's standing should own so little by way of quality furniture and possessions of any real value. On the domestic side, Westerdale, sitting at the kitchen table, could only note down a few sad old beds, a number of wooden tables and chairs, the vicar's desk, his books, the kitchen utensils, the pewter-ware, and precious little else, either by way of silver or other goods of substantial value.

The most notable items listed by the men were found outside the vicarage. These were the implements of husbandry, together with the livestock, the horses and the crops the field, which were soon due for harvesting. All these goods were duly added to the list in the presence of a scowling Adam, who, as Mary feared, did nothing to aid the task of the four men.

At last Thompson reappeared at the door of the vicarage.

'We've all done, Miss Mary. No need to disturb you further.'

''Tis no trouble, I assure you,' Mary replied.

The men respectfully touched their hats, and Mary watched them as they walked out of the yard.

'Good riddance to the lot of 'em,' Adam said savagely, emerging from the side of the house.

'They're only doing their duty,' Mary said softly. ''Tis done now and we'll not see them again.'

That evening the three occupants of the vicarage took their supper as usual around the kitchen table. There was little talk, each person deep in thought. The visit of the men had clearly shown that their time at the vicarage, a place that had been their home for so many years, was now drawing to a close.

True to her habit since the murder, Catherine soon took her leave and retired upstairs, leaving Mary and Adam sitting near the fire. Only one topic exercised their minds. What should they do? To stay at the vicarage was not possible. To stay at Owthorne was fraught with danger, but where were they to go?

'Folk around 'ere ain't gonna give up blabbin' about parson being done in,' Adam said in a resigned tone. 'They've naught else to talk about in this village.'

'I'm sure you're right, dearest. We have no choice but to leave Owthorne and go far away from all these people and their suspicions.'

'What about yer sister?' Adam asked, quickly warming to the notion of leaving the village he had hated since birth.

Mary fell silent for a moment; then her practical nature came to the fore. 'She must go elsewhere,' Mary answered with a determined voice. 'I shall miss my sister dearly, but we have each other. It is vital we go to a place where we are not known and no accusing fingers can be pointed at us. If needs be, we can take new names.'

Once more, silence reigned as the pair gazed into the now dying embers of the fire, deep in thought.

'I know,' Mary cried suddenly. 'Let's go to London!' Her face became bright with excitement at the idea, and she reached forward and put her hand on Adam's shoulder. 'Far away from everyone here,' she repeated. 'We'll marry soon enough at Halsham and leave without delay for London. But it must be our great secret. Not even Catherine must know of where we plan to go.'

Adam was of one mind with Mary's plan. With his old spirit of adventure rekindled, the vision of a new life in the distant metropolis, where he would no longer be the menial drudge, raised his spirits to a high level.

The next day Mary broached the subject of leaving the vicarage with Catherine. To Mary's great relief, her sister had no desire to stay in the village by the sea, with its dreaded secret and the patent animosity of almost all the people about her. Nevertheless, she had no wish to go to relatives at Kilham, nor, indeed, to leave the familiar rolling plain of Holderness. Eventually the two sisters decided to ask the Dunns at Patrington if Catherine could stay at the Manor House until such time as she could find a suitable place of her own in which to live.

The Manor House in North Street had been the home of George and Anne Dunn since their marriage well over twenty years before. Anne had died seven years ago, and the widower, George, had been looked after by his eldest daughter, Anne, until only last year when he too had passed away. Living now at the Manor House with Anne were her sister Mary, her brother George, and the twelve-year-old twins, James and Frances. Mary and Catherine Sinclare were well-known to the Dunn family, and relations had been extremely cordial over the years. The Sinclares felt sure that Anne Dunn, a young woman only slightly younger than Catherine herself, would offer the older girl a temporary home, and not allow the weight of local rumours to refuse them help in their hour of need. In this belief they were proved correct, for a short journey by the two sisters to Patrington a few days later was rewarded with an enthusiastic welcome from the young family there.

'We shall look after Catherine. She'll be one of the family. The twins will love her being with us,' Anne exclaimed, putting her arms lovingly around Catherine. 'We shall miss you sorely, Mary, but you must do whatever you think best.'

'I cannot thank you enough,' Mary replied, with genuine relief. 'What would we do without such good friends as the Dunns to help us in our hour of need? Of course, it will only be until Adam and I are truly established somewhere and can give a home again to my dear sister.'

'Where do you plan to go?' Anne enquired.

'Not sure yet,' Mary replied blandly. 'Somewhere north, perhaps.'

'I'm sure all will be well,' Anne concluded. 'And we'll wait to hear from you in due course.'

* * * * *

To the great relief of Mary and Adam, Samuel Prowde's third Sunday visit to Owthorne brought the news that Mr Sissison's licence was in the hands of Dr Fiddes. That clergyman, in turn, sent word via Prowde that the wedding could take place at Halsham at precisely half past eleven o'clock on the 29th of August. The choice of that day, a Sunday, surprised the couple, but upon discreet enquiry to Prowde they discovered that this would ensure an empty parish church, being well after the hour of the morning service, but comfortably before the Church's noon deadline for marriages.

Mary and Adam were delighted with the news. Now seemingly all the obstacles which had blocked their path to the altar were put aside. Mary counted out the silver coins necessary to pay the licence fee and handed them over to Prowde, together with her thanks for his assistance.

It was now the turn of Adam to make arrangements for the departure of Mary and himself from Owthorne. Four days before the wedding, he rode out alone from the vicarage, riding along the familiar route to Hull. With money grudgingly supplied by David Sinclare secured in one of the deep pockets of his leather breeches, he flaunted an evident air of confidence, indeed arrogance, revelling in his new-found station in life. After an uneventful journey, he steered his bay over the wooden beams of North Bridge, turned left through the North Gate and into the busy High Street of the town. At the far end of the street he espied the tall gateposts which led into the backyard of the King's Head inn.

'Quite the smart man about town now, ain't yer?' sneered Toby Joblin, the ostler's boy, his voice heavy with sarcasm. Adam ignored the lad's impudence and handed the sweating horse over to the care of the youth. Within minutes he was walking purposefully down Church Lane Staith and along the wooden pathway by the side of the river. His eyes carefully appraised each vessel moored, but on reaching North Bridge he felt disappointment at not finding a suitable boat for his purpose. He turned back, and when he had almost given up hope, he spotted a fine-looking Billy Boy, a two-masted vessel, some fifty or sixty feet in length, moored to a post by Blackfriars Gate. Adam knew from experience gained on previous visits that a vessel of this size was a 'coaster', and one which would regularly ply the route down to London. He carefully crossed the narrow bridge of planks which linked the boat's deck to the quayside, and putting his head into an open hatch, called loudly to attract the attention of anyone below deck. A few moments later a face, topped by a grey-coloured bonnet of wool, appeared at the opening.

'What do yer want?' the man said gruffly, as if annoyed to be disturbed from some precious moment of rest.

'I'm looking for two passages to London,' Adam began. 'We're to be wed o' Sunday, and we're leaving and wants to go to London. I'm willing to work m'passage.'

'Are you a sailor, then?' enquired the mariner.

'No,' Adam replied. 'But I can make myself as 'andy as any other feller 'ereabouts, an' m'wife can work the galley.'

We don't have no comforts for women aboard,' continued the mariner. 'I'm the master here. Henry Tolly's m'name. M'brother-in-law and his young lad make up m'crew. We've little enough space below for idle hands.'

'We'll not be idle, be assured,' Adam said quickly. 'D'you go regular to London from 'ere?'

'Aye, that we do. I'm off on the morrow's tide down the Trent to pick up some lead pigs, and back 'ere to take on some bags of milled flour, all for London.'

'We can sleep on the flour bags,' Adam said quickly. He was now becoming desperate, wanting to secure places on board the boat. 'We'll be no trouble. We can pay for our passages and work as needs be.'

'I don't know,' the mariner said slowly, looking at Adam. 'We don't normally take folk, and it's a rough life at sea, special like for a young woman.'

'My Mary won't mind. She'll work in the galley for you.' Adam's feelings of desperation were now becoming plain to see, but he had the sense to try a new tack.

'When do you sail next for London?' he asked.

'High tide on the first day of September.'

There was a long pause whilst the mariner moved his head

slowly from side to side, as if reluctant to make a firm decision. At length and to Adam's great relief, the mariner capitulated.

'All right, I'll take you. You can both make yourselves useful, but I still wants two sovereigns from each o' you and before we sails, in m'hand.'

Adam gave a grunt of acceptance and the deal was sealed with a firm handshake.

'We'll be 'ere in good time,' Adam said. 'You'll 'ave your money first thing.'

Adam returned to the quayside with feelings within him of both relief and pleasure at securing the means of their escape from Holderness. But he had one more task to accomplish before setting back on the road to Owthorne. Returning to the inn, he entered the stables in search of the ostler. He soon found his man, a red-faced individual, some fifty years of age, of broad girth, who was examining the coat of a large chestnut mare which had just been brushed by his stable boy.

'I 'ears you buys and sells 'osses,' Adam said without bothering to introduce himself.

'Could do,' replied the ostler cautiously. 'Not a good time for buying right now, coming on for autumn it ain't.'

'I'm back 'ere on the first of September, sailing on the tide to London, with m'wife. I've yon bay to sell, a fine animal, and a dapple grey of fifteen hands as well. I'm wanting to sell 'em 'fore we go on board.'

'Didn't know as you was wed,' the ostler rejoined quizzically, keeping his gaze continuously on the chestnut. He was a man who kept well informed of local gossip, and the tale of the missing vicar, who had been a frequent visitor at the inn, was well known in the town. 'How do I know they're yours to sell?'

'The horses belong to Mistress Mary Sinclare, my late master's niece. We're getting wed on Sunday.'

The ostler sniffed deeply. He wiped his nose with a swift horizontal motion of his coat sleeve, and then his brow with a similar movement in the reverse direction. 'Saddles, reins 'n all?'

'Saddles an' all,' replied Adam.

'Yonder bay, I'll give you fifteen sovereigns,' said the ostler with an added sniff of the nose.

'She's worth a lot more than that,' Adam retorted sharply.

'Like as I says, it's not a good time right now, and I'll not put a price on the grey till I've seen her.'

'Dammit, I wants twenty pounds for the bay. It goes with the saddle and 'arness,' Adam said truculently.

'Lord, I couldn't turn a 'alfpenny on that price. Like as not I'd lose money on the deal.'

The ostler seemed immovable, but Adam argued a few minutes more, and eventually was obliged to settle for seventeen pounds, the best price that he could force from the ostler.

'An' I expect to see the same animal back 'ere on the first. No trickery or there'll not be a penny from me,' was the ostler's final remark, turning away from Adam and back to the chestnut horse.

Adam felt thoroughly disgruntled as he strode over to his horse, held ready by the stable boy. Ignoring the boy's outstretched hand, anticipating the customary gratuity, Adam dug his heels into the horse's flanks and steered the animal out of the inn's yard and northwards along High Street.

'A fine animal like this, for seventeen poxy pounds!' Adam mouthed these words savagely several times as he journeyed along the Holderness Road. After a time, however, and on deeper reflection, he consoled himself that the most important part of his mission had been accomplished. All was now in place, both for his marriage to Mary and for their escape from Holderness.

Chapter Eight

The grey skies of the morning of Sunday, the 29th of August soon gave way to shafts of bright sunlight, and the appearance of blue skies between white clouds. To avert all suspicion, Mary, Catherine and Adam took up their usual places in St Peter's, and patiently followed the now familiar style of service conducted by Samuel Prowde. The curate, for his part, had promised to maintain a strict silence regarding their plans for the wedding. After morning service, in the solitude of the vicarage, he gave Mary and Adam his blessing on their life together, as he put it, 'wherever that may be.' His departure from the vicarage was followed within minutes by three mounted figures en route for Halsham. On the Sabbath day, clad in their Sunday best, the trio passed almost unnoticed as they left the vicarage on their short journey.

On arrival, the riders were met at the cottage near the church by the rector's wife. Mary was taken aback by the kindness of Jane Fiddes, who escorted the sisters into her chamber to tidy and prepare for the nuptials. To Mary's surprise and pleasure, the rector's wife had cut sprigs of rosemary, which she carefully attached to the sleeves of the dresses worn by Mary and Catherine.

'There,' she exclaimed. 'Let God bless this happy occasion.'

Mary gripped the arm of Jane Fiddes in a silent gesture of thanks. It had felt so long since she had received such kindness from an outsider, or experienced real happiness, the events of recent weeks having excluded all such human emotions.

'Thank you, my dear,' she said at last. 'I'm ready. Let us not keep your husband waiting.'

'And yours to be,' added Jane, giving a gentle smile to Mary.

Keeping their eyes firmly fixed on Adam and Dr Fiddes, waiting in the chancel of the church, the three women advanced along the nave, joining the men in front of the Lord's table. At their rear, and almost unnoticed, the group was joined by the rector's son, Dick.

The responses which Mary and Adam gave in turn were the only variations in sound from the deep tones of the rector as he went through the familiar phrases of the marriage ceremony. Individually, the secret thoughts of the two sisters followed similar paths, each contemplating the irony of the present situation, so different from the many occasions they had witnessed at St Peter's, when their uncle had presided over nuptials. For Adam, no such deep thoughts or flights of emotion troubled his mind. The wages of his crime were clear and immediate. His marriage to Mary had broken the chains of his former life of servitude, and to leave this hated place now became the sole object of his desire.

After the wedding, and to the continued surprise of the trio from Owthorne, the rector invited them into his cottage, where a cup of wine, made warm by the fireside, was waiting. This drink was accompanied by slices of Jane's oatcake, spread with butter. Mary was happier than she had been in weeks. Even the fact that she had been obliged to supply her own ring, an old band of sorts found in a drawer at the vicarage, did not quench her high spirits as she clung to Adam's arm. Neither did she give much thought or concern for the quiet demeanour of Catherine, who only joined in the conversation when directly spoken to, and whose pallid complexion seemed to Mary to be little out of the ordinary.

At last the three visitors bade the Fiddes family farewell and retraced the steps of their journey back to Owthorne. There was much to do. It had been arranged with the Dunns that Catherine would join them the next day. For this, Adam needed to commandeer one of the farm wains from Jordan to transport two wooden trunks, which contained the young woman's clothes and her few possessions, to the Manor House at Patrington. Mary opted not to accompany Adam and her sister on this journey, but conducted a tearful farewell inside the vicarage. The sisters embraced and exchanged promises to write to each other. Mary, ever determined and practical, had one last vital mission to conclude.

'Sister, dear,' she said, 'pray do not ever forget your solemn oath given on the Holy Book, that you will never tell a living soul what has happened here, and what became of uncle.'

Through her tears and spasms of coughing, the now quite distraught younger sister weakly nodded her assent. Mary, however, was not satisfied with this sign, and it was only when Catherine was able to speak her faint words of promise that Mary released the grip on her sister's shoulders. After a final embrace, Mary helped Catherine up on the front of the wain beside Adam. She watched the two figures slowly recede into the distance until out of sight along the road. As she did, she could not help but notice that Catherine made no attempt to look back or wave in any gesture of sisterly farewell. Mary returned to the house with an uncomfortable feeling of unease. It was clear that her future happiness and that of her husband rested solely in the hands of her sister, upon whom she was obliged to trust with their lives. It was imperative, she thought, that they must quickly find a place to live in London, where they would not be recognised and where they could begin a new life, whatever the pain or cost involved.

Later that afternoon, when Adam returned from Patrington, he found that Mary had gathered together essential items of clothing and personal belongings she wished to carry to London. The next day, the 31st August, was to be their last at the vicarage.

Adam immediately began to comb through the house, intent on taking articles of value that he could sell, but Mary became alarmed.

'Adam! Dearest. No! It would be folly to take even the smallest spoon,' she said. 'All the silver and whatever else here has been listed, and Uncle David will not take kindly for any loss. We must travel light to London. I have some money put by, and we shall not starve.' She touched him tenderly on the cheek. 'It will be hard, no doubt, but we have each other, and I know we shall find employment.'

Adam stopped his foraging and turned to Mary.

'After all we've done for that wretched, ungrateful man, it seems only right we should 'elp ourselves to a picking or two. It's not fair that your Uncle David at Kilham should 'ave all this, when 'e's done nothing to deserve it and 'ardly ever shown 'is face 'ere.'

But Mary was firm. 'Dearest. We must only take away what truly belongs to us. Rumours are bad enough already about Uncle Henock, so we don't want to add to our troubles by being called thieves.'

Irritably Adam pulled away from her. 'We need it more than your Uncle David,' he argued, but then he shrugged his shoulders and reluctantly acquiesced. 'But if that's 'ow it's to be, I suppose it's for the best.'

After supper Adam went out to the stables and Mary settled down to write a letter to David Sinclare. She hesitated over how to word it, not wanting to alarm him or give away their future plans. By the time she had finished writing the letter it was quite dark. In candlelight she read through the letter carefully, making sure she had not left out any important details.

'Dear Uncle David,' the letter began. 'I have much news to impart and ask your forgiveness that I must tell you by letter rather than coming myself to Kilham. I am pleased to say that I am now married to Adam, and after all the terrible troubles of the past weeks, we have decided to leave the vicarage and make a new start for ourselves, away from Holderness. Catherine has gone to stay with good friends at Patrington. No doubt, soon enough she will decide where she wants to live in the future. The keys of the vicarage are with Jordan, and he will look after the land and the animals for as long as you wish him to do so. I know you will settle with him and treat him kindly, as he has been a true and faithful servant to Uncle Henock these past twelve years. I beg your indulgence for taking the bay, which Adam needs for the journey. You may recall that the grey was a gift to me last year from Uncle Henock. Please be assured that I shall write again to let you know we are safe and well.'

After reading through the letter, Mary gave a slight nod of approval to herself, and ended the page with, 'I remain your affectionate niece, Mary Sinclare', before sealing the letter with wax and the aid of a nearby candle.

Mary then called in Jordan to give him his final instructions. He listened, saying little, and showed no surprise on learning of Mary's intentions. For all that Mary and Adam had taken care to keep their wedding and plans to leave a secret, the villagers had watched their comings and goings from behind half-closed shutters, and correctly sized up the situation.

Finally, Mary said, 'One more thing, John.' She picked up the letter from the table. 'Will you give this to Will and ask him to deliver it to Kilham tomorrow. It is most important.'

'If all goes to plan,' she thought to herself, 'we will be safely at sea by the time Uncle David receives it.'

At seven sharp next morning Jordan was waiting in the yard of the vicarage. Adam was the first to emerge from the house, and he gave Jordan a curt nod of his head in brusque acknowledgement of his presence as he passed by on the way to the stables. A few minutes later Adam led out two horses, saddled and ready for the journey. Beckoning to Jordan to hold the reins, Adam went back into the house, re-emerging with two large cloth bundles, which he secured to the sides of his bay mare. A few moments later Mary came out of the house, locked the door behind her and handed the key over to Jordan.

'I'm sorry to see you leave 'n all, Mistress, and wish you good fortune wherever you may go.'

'Thank you, John,' Mary replied. 'I'll miss seeing you each

day, that's for sure. You have served my uncle and us well and truly all these years past.'

Jordan helped Mary up into the saddle and stood back a pace. He ignored Adam, who had already mounted, but instinctively touched the brim of his straw hat in salute to Mary, and gave her horse a firm slap on the rump. Mary followed Adam out through the yard gates and along the village road, and following the example of her sister, she too was determined not to look back. In doing so, she ignored the accusing stares of the some of the village women who stood by their cottage doors.

'Good riddance!' Adam shouted over his shoulder as they turned into the Hull road. Both riders broke into a gentle canter. 'We'll be aboard by ten,' he cried triumphantly.

'God be praised,' Mary added, her eyes intent on the road ahead, not caring to admire the golden coloured fields on either side, patterned by clumps of sheaves of wheat or barley. Neither did she care to look at the men working amongst the corn.

Their spirits rose with each passing mile, and it seemed to them that their journey represented a passage out from a dark nightmare into the bright dream of a new beginning.

A little later then Adam had predicted, the pair turned their horses out of Hull's High Street and trotted down a narrow street towards the river Hull. Ahead of them the masts of the Billy Boy came into view. To Mary's inexperienced eyes, the boat, shorn of sail with bare masts and criss-crossed rigging, appeared like some leafless tree in winter. The vessel was firmly resting on the mud of the bed of the river, but Adam was quick to notice that the tide was already entering the river from the Humber.

The quayside was a hive of activity. A waggon, coupled to two motionless cart horses, stood opposite the ship's lifting tackle. Two men inside the waggon were loading hundred-weight sacks of corn into a sling, and Adam watched as Henry Tolly expertly manoeuvred the sling over the side of the Billy Boy and lowered it into a hatch and out of sight. Below deck, Adam imagined that the master's brother-in-law and their young deckhand would be busy stowing the sacks.

Adam and Mary dismounted. Adam untied the bags from his horse, bundles which now represented the total of all their worldly goods, and laid them on the quayside. Tolly greeted their arrival with a perfunctory wave, which barely interrupted the rhythm of his hand movements working the tackle.

'Be so good as to stay on shore till we've loaded up,' the master called.

Adam noticed two more waggons waiting to be unloaded behind the first. 'Wait here, m'dear,' he said. 'You'll be safe o'er there whilst I go off to sell the 'osses.'

Adam remounted his horse, and leading Mary's grey by the reins, rode off in the direction of High Street. Mary sat down on a nearby bench to wait, guarding the bundles placed around her feet. The strangeness of the situation continued to flood her mind. Although now in her mid-twenties, and having spent most of her life by the sea, she realised that she'd never before been on a sea-going craft larger than a small fishing boat. In a life of semi-gentility at the vicarage she'd not mixed with sea-going folk, other than the Handsons, who fished from the small bay at Tunstall. Now, she thought, 'I'm about to embark on a voyage to the City of London, a place I've never seen.'

She raised her head to view the scene, breathed in the salt air, and blotting out from her mind all the past events which had brought her to this situation, she felt an unmistakable thrill of pleasure. This was indeed 'the greatest adventure', to be shared with the man she loved. Whatever the coming hardships, Mary thought, she was determined to play her part to the full.

Adam guided the two horses to the High Street, through the gates of the King's Head and into the familiar surroundings of the inn's cobbled yard. Bringing the horses to a standstill, he dismounted and, with an imperious wave of the hand, brushed aside a stable-boy's offer to take the reins.

'Go fetch me Tom Bradley. Quickly, m'lad,' he brusquely demanded of the boy.

Tom Bradley, the ostler at the King's Head, came into view at the inn's back door.

'Oh, it's you again,' he said, with little enthusiasm. 'What do you want now?'

'I've two 'osses to sell,' Adam told him. 'I want the seventeen sovereigns for the bay and twelve for the grey.'

'Do you now!' exclaimed Bradley, with mock surprise.

The ostler looked Adam up and down, and then did the same for the horses. He examined the mouth of each horse, and then, bending down, he ran his hands over their fetlocks.

Straightening his back again, he gave an audible sniff of the nose and proceeded to wipe that member on the cuff of his coat.

'Not worth that much,' he said to Adam.

'What! Course they are!' Adam blustered. 'A bargain at that price. To be sure, if I'd time to wait I could get twice the money.'

'Not from me you couldn't,' said Bradley truculently. 'I'll give you the seventeen for the bay as agreed, and eight for the grey.'

'Aw, come on,' Adam said. 'You can do better than that. That's good horse flesh there.' He gave the grey a firm thwack on the flank. 'You'll not find better anywhere abouts 'ere.'

Bradley said nothing, and Adam began to feel desperate.

'Like I said afore,' Adam said. 'I'll throw in the saddles 'n all for thirty pounds.'

'Oh, would you indeed?' Bradley exclaimed with a sneer. 'My last price is 26 pounds, 'osses, saddles, tackle, the lot. Tak it or leave it.'

Adam flushed with anger. He wanted to punch the man for his dogmatic attitude and, above all, for his refusal to pay a fair price. Bitterly, he realised that the ostler would not give more, and as he was in no position to take the horses away, he was obliged to accept Bradley's low offer. Defeated and angry, he snatched the twenty-six gold coins from the ostler's outstretched hand and stalked out of the yard.

When Adam returned to the quayside, he was in a black temper. Mary stood up and patiently listened whilst Adam raged about his dealings with Bradley at the inn. Mary put her arms around her husband and did her best to soothe him.

'It's not your fault,' she said. 'Don't be angry. You had no choice, my love. It's done now, and what do a few less coins matter now?'

Mary held Adam in her arms, but at that point she noticed that the master was beckoning to them from the boat.

'Come aboard now, if you please,' Tolly called out. 'We're all stowed away.'

Fully distracted from his grievance, Adam picked up the two bundles, and they walked towards an angled gangway of planks which bridged the quayside to the Billy Boy.

Mary was first to reach the deck, having gingerly negotiated the hazardous walkway of planks, her last steps being supported by Tolly's outstretched hand. Adam followed Mary onto the ship, carrying one bundle over each shoulder.

'Take 'em down below,' ordered Tolly, pointing to the bundles.

'We'll be leaving shortly on the turn of the tide.'

Adam nodded and began to descend through a narrow hatch, down a steep wooden staircase. The narrowness of the opening, however, caused Adam some difficulty in squeezing the bundles after him. To the master's undisguised amusement, Mary assisted Adam by pushing the bundles through the hatch with her foot.

Mary's curiosity led her to follow Adam, to explore what lay below. At first she had difficulty in picking out the geography of these new surroundings, but after a few moments her eyes became accustomed to the half-light. To her surprise, there were no partitions, cabins or divisions to be seen dividing the space. It was a single, large open area running from the bow to the stern, only interrupted by the stout circular bases of the masts sprouting from the floor of the hull and piercing the deck above.

Covering over half of the area lay the cargo, where the master's brother-in-law and a fresh-faced lad of about eleven or twelve were busy completing the task of evenly stowing away the last few sacks of corn. The man greeted the two newcomers with a perfunctory, 'Good day to you,' touching the brim of his hat in salute, but without breaking off from the job in hand.

At the other end of the hold Mary spotted a small galley, together with a stove, an assortment of cupboards, benches and a stout table. This was clearly the living area, she thought, surveying the scene with some dismay at the basic conditions which were to be her home for the next few days. They did not linger below for long, and after Adam had deposited the bundles beside the table, they climbed back onto the upper deck to await the ship's departure.

Mary and Adam watched with keen interest as the master and crew made preparations to leave the harbour. By now the water level had risen to the high tide mark, allowing the vessel to float freely, and with the swirling movement of the water, she was straining at the mooring ropes. Imperceptibly, two small rowing boats appeared at the stern; ropes were flung across and lines secured between the vessel and the rowing boats. With the rowers pulling in unison on their oars, the Billy Boy slowly but surely began to reverse out of the river and into the Humber.

When clear of the land, the towing lines were released, and the rowers called out cheery goodbyes and 'God speed' as they returned to the quayside. Sails were raised, and with the master at the wheel, expertly tacking to take advantage of the wind, the vessel began to follow a course eastwards along the Humber towards the sea.

Mary and Adam held each other tightly. No words were exchanged, but both fully absorbed, they watched as behind them the tower of Holy Trinity church in the Market Place of Hull began to recede into the distance. Their escape from Holderness had been achieved. The dark events of recent months, which had brought them to such a low ebb, now began to fade, as warm feelings of relief and thoughts of a new life together flooded their minds and bodies.

Chapter Nine

The days at sea proved to be idyllic ones for the two lovers. It was almost as though the past dark days in Holderness had never taken place. Adam's old passion for life at sea returned, and Mary had never seen him look so happy and so animated. Her new husband responded with enthusiasm to all the master's instructions, and was soon engrossed in sharing the work of handling the sails and rigging, together with the other men. As Adam became a useful crew member, so too did the master's attitude of reserve soften, and he became more accommodating to the two passengers. They soon learnt that Henry Tolly, a man in his late forties, hailed from York, where his wife kept a beer-house in Monkgate and cared for their four children. Tolly's mate and brother-in-law was called John Hutton, and John's young son, Thomas, the cabin boy, made up the crew of the Billy Boy.

Mary and Adam feared that they would be obliged to bed down at night on sacks of corn, but much to Mary's relief, Tolly produced two hammocks, which once they had mastered the knack of lying within them, proved to be tolerable substitutes for their customary beds.

Tolly soon perceived that Mary was a woman of some breeding and did his best to provide her with a little privacy for washing and dressing. Although he went to some trouble to rig up a canvas sheet across one corner of the open cabin space, he still apologised to her for the basic nature of the domestic facilities he had on board. In respect of ablutions, all Tolly could provide were two buckets, one for washing after drawing water from a large wooden barrel stored near the galley, and the other for nature's needs, which after use was let down over the side and washed out with seawater. To Mary's secret amusement, she never espied any of her new companions washing in any visible way, and noted that the procedure on retirement for sleep at the end of the day was limited to the sole act of removing their boots.

Aided by a fair wind and enjoying full sail, the Billy Boy made good progress in her journey southwards. Tolly left the duty at the wheel to his crew, but regularly kept a check on the ship's course, using his traverse board and compass. Throughout the day he ensured that the boat stayed within sight of the Lincolnshire coast on the starboard side. As night approached, and with daylight fading, he brought her even closer to land before dropping anchor. Warning lamps, fuelled by colza oil, were lit and secured to the tops of each mast, fore and aft, and then all would take their ease until the first light of the next day.

Mary, not to be outdone in making herself useful, took charge of the galley. Young Thomas Hutton was only too pleased to be relieved of this irksome task, and was enthusiastic in showing Mary all the equipment needed for her new-found duties. Cooking was, Mary thought, a very grand term for the rather plain and monotonous menu served on board the Billy Boy. The solitary cooking utensil perched high on the stove was a large iron skillet covered by a lid. Under the lid Mary saw a bubbling stew with lumps of mutton or rabbit reinforced with a hearty variety of vegetables: beans, carrots, peas and onions. After each serving, which was eaten from deeply indented pewter plates with pewter spoons, the volume of stew was restored to the high point mark by tossing in new chunks of salted meat and fresh vegetables, and the whole topped up with water from a barrel. This concoction then remained on the stove throughout the day, simmering like some witch's brew.

Mary soon learnt that the water she used for washing in also served for cooking purposes, although, thankfully she thought, not for drinking. The crew drank small beer, which was stored in a number of casks in a corner of the galley. For this, Mary was kept busy at meal times filling and refilling their tin tankards, proffered at frequent intervals during the evening meal.

Mary also learnt that the beer had a secondary culinary purpose, in that by the second day out from Hull, the bread taken on board was so hard that it required to be dipped in the beer to render it edible.

Mealtimes over, the company would sit around the table, content to drink more beer. Tolly and John Hutton smoked their clay pipes and occasionally John played a few tunes on his penny whistle.

'What are you folks going to do in London?' Tolly asked during a lull in the entertainment.

'Find a place to stay whilst we look for work,' replied Mary. 'For I'm sure London's an expensive place, and our money will soon be gone.'

'What'll you do?'

'You could take me on board,' said Adam suddenly. 'You can see I'm fit for work 'ere.'

Mary shot an alarmed glance at Adam. She had no desire to be left alone in a strange city, and she instantly saw the danger of Adam returning frequently to Hull, albeit as a seaman on a ship. It was with some relief that she heard Tolly say that for the present he had no need of an extra pair of hands.

'At least I can see you put up at lodgings near where we berth,' Tolly continued. 'I goes there myself, while John and Tom stays on here, working the cargo. Mistress Ashley's a fine woman. She keeps a clean house and a good table. Pretty reasonable terms too – for friends of mine,' he added jovially, giving his passengers a knowing wink, and pushing his empty tankard in Mary's direction.

The second day out from Hull saw the Billy Boy sailing across the wide mouth of the Wash. It was a long haul to the Norfolk coast, but at last the dark outlines of Blakeney harbour and a few faint lights on the quayside came within sight, before Tolly gave the command to drop anchor.

'Tomorrow we'll anchor at Yarmouth. John and Tom can go ashore and bring us back some tasty food and fresh beer. Perhaps a few pies as well, to celebrate our good fortune!'

Tolly was obviously in high spirits and slapped Tom on the back. The boy merely nodded and went to join his father and Adam in the work of gathering in the sails for the night.

The thought of going ashore the next day rather appealed to Mary, and she conjured up visions of how she imagined the town of Yarmouth to be. Doubtless, she thought, it must be a busy place, with many shops, taverns and new sights to see.

'I should like to go ashore too,' Mary said to Tolly.

'Begging your pardon, mistress,' Tolly replied. 'But it ain't possible for a lady such as yourself. You see, we don't go in to tie up as we does at Hull. We stay outside the harbour, and we needs John and Tom to do the work for us fetching and carrying.'

'I don't mind lending a hand,' Mary persisted, but Tolly was adamant in his refusal to accommodate her request.

'You'll see what I'm talking about soon enough,' he replied, and ended the conversation by way of pushing his empty tankard once more towards Mary.

The next day, and exactly as Tolly had told Mary, the Billy Boy dropped anchor outside the harbour wall at Great Yarmouth. Mary could only watch as the Huttons lowered a rowing boat over the side of their ship and clambered down a rope ladder slung from the deck to the small boat. Mary and Adam watched as the pair rowed away from the Billy Boy, soon to disappear through an opening in the harbour wall and out of sight.

With Tolly engaged elsewhere, Mary and Adam were left alone on deck. Mary was still worried about Adam's continued desire to go to sea, and felt obliged to take advantage of a few quiet moments together to warn Adam of the perils of such a course of action.

'Dearest,' she began. 'We can never go back to Yorkshire, not even to return to Hull on a boat. It's far too dangerous.'

'What's to fear there now?' Adam asked.

'You know that I love my sister Catherine and shall surely miss her company in London. But we must always be on our guard. She is the only other person in this world who knows what took place on that day at the vicarage. If she was to reveal what happened, the law would hound us down and destroy our happiness.'

'You made 'er swear on the Bible not to tell a soul what we done,' Adam countered truculently. 'Don't it matter to 'er?'

'Indeed it does,' Mary replied. 'It's true she swore a solemn oath on the Holy Bible, but you know she's a weak and poorly girl. I fear that under a fierce cross-examination she might well succumb and tell all. No, dearest, we may never go back to Hull,' she said gently. 'For better or worse, we must make a new life for ourselves in London. I'll find work too, however hard, and we'll succeed, you see if we don't.'

'If I can't go to sea,' said Adam dourly, 'what can I do in a big city like London? I've never been further than 'ull in all m'life.'

'Courage, sweetheart,' Mary rejoined. 'Your skill with the horses will find good employment. Take heart, all will be well.'

Mary slipped her arm around Adam and silently prayed that she had reassured him. 'All will be well, you'll see,' she repeated, and alone on the deck the two embraced and kissed.

After an hour or so Tolly appeared on deck, refreshed from a quiet nap below. The three figures leant, side-by-side, on the rails of the Billy Boy watching the comings and goings at the harbour. After a time they saw a rowing boat emerge from the harbour and two familiar figures came into view. Tolly carefully raised the new provisions, hauling them up in a sling, whilst Mary and Adam busied themselves carrying boxes of food and small casks of beer below. That night the five on board enjoyed a hearty meal of beef pies and hot vegetables from the ubiquitous stew pot, together with fresh bread, all washed down with some lively Suffolk strong ale. Even Tom, who was usually a silent companion at the table, joined in with after-supper singing to the accompaniment of lilting notes from his father's whistle. All slept soundly that night.

Blessed by fair weather and a favourable breeze, the Billy Boy continued to make good progress along the Essex coastline. Evening halts outside Harwich and Shoeburyness were accomplished without incident, and after five days at sea, Tolly was able to announce that they had entered the Thames estuary.

Mary spent much of her time on deck and felt a growing sense of excitement as the northern and southern banks of the river slowly began to close in on the Billy Boy. She noted a considerable increase in river traffic, which was in marked contrast to the few vessels that had saluted them when crossing their path on the journey south from Lincolnshire.

Tolly had now taken over command at the wheel, and speed was reduced by hauling down a pair of the mainsails. It was not long before the river banks, which hitherto had been covered by greenery and trees, were now occupied by warehouses and quays. Ships and barges of all sizes were both moored or sailing up and down on each side of the river, causing Mary to admire Tolly's skill in finding a clear course through the maze of shipping,

'The city of London,' shouted Tolly. 'A fine view, to be sure,' he added, pointing ahead to pick out the shining white stone walls of St Paul's cathedral. 'Some forty years ago, the old 'un burnt down and this 'n's bran' new. Most of the city an' all. You'll never see the like anywhere else in the world!'

Mary and Adam merely nodded back, fascinated by the view, and with growing feelings of excitement. To her delight, Mary recognised a building, the drawing of which she had seen in a book in her uncle's library.

'The tower of London,' she cried, as the tall, square stone structure, capped by towers at each corner and surrounded by stone walls, came clearly into view.

'I'm heading for Hay's Wharf,' said Tolly. 'I alus goes there and they keeps a tidy berth ready for me.'

At that point Adam was beckoned away by John Hutton to assist with furling the remaining sails. Tolly locked the wheel with a curiously shaped piece of wood, and within minutes two rowing boats joined the Billy Boy, with their occupants calling out warm greetings to Tolly. Tom threw out lines fore and aft, and in a manner reminiscent of their departure from the river Hull, but in reverse order, the Billy Boy was pulled in to the quayside and secured fast.

'There,' cried Tolly to nobody in particular. 'The good ship reaches her port in safety. God be praised!'

'Amen,' thought Mary, and at a bidding from Tolly, she went below to put together their belongings.

It was late afternoon before Tolly signalled to Mary and Adam it was time to leave the Billy Boy.

'John and Tom'll be staying aboard,' Tolly advised. 'We're off to find Mistress Ashley in Magdalen Street. Another fine port o' call,' he added with a laugh.

It was now time to leave, but for all that the sight of London excited her, Mary reflected how much she had enjoyed the days at sea. The voyage had served as a calming distraction, helping to eradicate from her mind the terrible events back at the vicarage. In addition, during the time at sea, she had grown fond of young Tom and felt sad that it was now time to part.

'You can have your galley back,' Mary said, giving Tom a warm hug, a gesture which caused the boy some embarrassment, standing, as he was, beside his father. John Hudson merely gave a casual wave of farewell to the pair.

'Good luck to you both in London,' he said. 'Sure enough we'll see you again on t'next trip.'

'I hope not,' mused Mary, and restricted her reply to calling back, 'A safe return to Hull.' With that she turned away and followed Tolly over the gangplank and onto the quayside.

Mary found her first steps on dry land a strange experience. 'I feel as though I'm drunk!' she cried, and turned to hold onto Adam, who was following close behind, carrying the bundles of clothes.

'You'll soon get used to that,' laughed Tolly, as he led them away from the dock area. Adam looked back wistfully and gave an audible sigh when they turned a corner and the bare masts of the Billy Boy disappeared from view.

'Soon be at Mistress Ashley's,' said Tolly, 'an' a good hot supper with plenty of meat to cheer us up, no doubt.'

True to his word, Tolly was soon knocking on the door of a house situated roughly in the middle of a row of identical buildings down a narrow street. Mary cast her eye along the houses and noted that beside each front door was a single window, and this feature was matched by another on the upper floor. With two stone steps leading up to the door, and a round metal manhole lid in the pavement, which Mary presumed led to some sort of coal cellar, there was nothing to distinguish Mistress Ashley's lodging house from any of those adjoining, or, for that matter, any facing on the opposite side of the road. Her nose quickly picked up the unmistakeable smell of garbage, which lay about the granite sets of the street.

'The fire didn't reach here, thank God,' Tolly said to Mary, as if to explain away some unspoken question. 'Come on woman,' he said to the closed door, in a mock tone of impatience.

It was Mistress Ashley herself who finally opened the door. She was a buxom, jolly woman of about forty years, with apple-red cheeks, plainly enhanced by some red powder. She greeted Tolly warmly and waited for him to make the introductions.

'Bessy,' said Tolly. 'These good people have sailed with me from Hull. They wedded recently and have come to try their luck in your fair city. I've told 'em of your kind hospitality.'

Mistress Ashley gave a broad smile of welcome and executed an exaggerated bob of a curtsy to greet the two newcomers. Then taking Mary's arm, she escorted the party into the house.

'Welcome to my little house, my dears. I'll see you right, here. I have a room free upstairs, and although I says it myself, my lodgings with a full meat supper at only one shilling and sixpence per night is the best and most reasonable you'll find in these parts of London.'

Bessy Ashley led Mary and Adam up a short flight of stairs. At the top a single door led into a bedroom, in which was a large bed, an ottoman, a chest of drawers complete with mirror above, and a padded chair.

'This is my room, dears,' she said with an airy wave of the hand. 'Yorn is through here. How long were you thinking of staying?'

Mary and Adam followed the wide sweep of Bessy Ashley's skirt as she opened another door on the far side of the bedroom.

'You'll be snug in here, my dears. I'm up and about at six o' the morn and I'll bring you up some hot water at six-thirty sharp. How long did you say you were staying?'

Mary, who had had little chance to make any reply to the continuous chatter from her hostess, gave a quick glance to Adam, but he merely shrugged his shoulders.

'It will depend, Mistress Ashley, on how quickly we find work,' Mary said. 'We will begin to make some enquiries in the morning.'

'Indeed you must, my dears. London soon runs away with your money, but we may be able to help on that score. My nephew Will is joining us for supper. He's a carrier by trade, and keeps a sharp eye on what goes on in the city.' She turned to Adam. 'Hoping you won't object, sir,' she said, 'but I needs half-a-sovereign in advance, as it were, with all the victuals to buy in, you see.'

Adam looked at Mary for help. With Mistress Ashley's imposing form stationed by her side and with her hand held out, Mary had little option but to take out her purse and hand over a small gold coin.

'Thank you most kindly,' their hostess beamed. 'You'll be very snug here. Just married, did you say? Supper's in the parlour, seven-ish, just as soon as my Will comes.' With that, Mistress Ashley was gone, closing the bedroom door behind her. Mary looked at Adam, first with a degree of resignation, and then she broke into gentle laughter.

Welcome to the city of London and Mistress Ashley,' she said to Adam with a broad smile on her face.

'Some woman!' Adam sighed. 'I wonder where Mr Ashley is? Away at sea, if he has any sense, I shouldn't wonder.'

Mary and Adam left their bedroom promptly at seven o'clock. As they passed through the room of their hostess and onto the stairs, they were greeted by a delicious smell emanating from below. Adam breathed in the wafting aroma deeply, then slowly expelled the air from his lungs.

'Perhaps London ain't so bad after all,' he said to Mary with a smile. 'Tolly's brought us some good luck at last.'

'Never doubt it, dearest,' Mary responded. 'We shall do well here, just you see. Let's go down and see what Mistress Ashley can put on the table.'

The pair presented themselves in what was clearly a parlour-cum-kitchen. Tolly was sitting in a high-backed settle, positioned to the right of a large open fire. In his left hand he held a short clay pipe, whilst his right secured a tankard of ale. Unbeknown to Mary and Adam, Henry Tolly had not moved from this comfortable place for nigh on two hours, but had contentedly puffed on his pipe and drunk his fill, watching Mistress Ashley busy herself about the kitchen.

'Come on in,' Tolly called rather grandly, waving his pipe in their direction. 'I hope you're good and hungry!'

This last remark caused the two guests to observe several iron pots suspended over the fire, and immediately in front, on a spit, was skewered a large joint of beef. To accompany the delicious smell, a comforting, sizzling noise came from the roast meat, and a steady drip of hot fat fell from the joint and was captured in a long iron tray placed beneath.

It was soon evident to Mary and Adam that Tolly and Bessy Ashley were on very familiar terms of friendship. They could not help but notice the fondly exchanged looks and the intimate strokes of the hand which the woman gave to the mariner's head and shoulders whenever she passed by the end of the settle.

Almost at once there was a knock on the door, and without waiting to be ushered in, Will Ashley came into the room. He tossed his hat upon the stairs and planted a firm kiss on his aunt's cheek. Turning round, Will spotted Tolly sitting on the settle. 'There you are, you old seadog!' he cried, moving forward to give Tolly a firm but friendly pat on the shoulder. 'I see we've visitors, too. Who do we have 'ere, 'enry?'

With a grunt Tolly rose from his seat by the fire and made the introductions.

'From up north, eh?' Will exclaimed. 'No doubt come to London to seek your fortune. Don't believe what they say about the streets 'ere being paved w'gold. I can tell you fer sure, they ain't. That's right, isn't it, 'enry?'

Tolly nodded sagely. 'But come all,' he cried. 'Sit at table, whilst I do justice to that fine looking piece of beef.'

Bessy Ashley motioned to Mary, Adam and Will to sit down at the oak table, which occupied the central area of the room. Tolly carefully removed the joint from the spit and placed it on a wooden trencher. Whilst he was carving, Bessy added suet dumplings to pewter places, and placed a large pot containing vegetables cooked in a rich gravy, coloured by small pieces of overdone meat, on the table.

'Help yourselves, good people,' she said, removing her apron and sitting down at the table next to her nephew.

For a while there was little conversation, as all set to, giving full justice to Mistress Ashley's culinary hospitality. Eventually the silence was broken by Tolly, who, raising his tankard, cried, 'Here's a health to our young couple here. Good fortune attend them in this great city!'

As the tankards were refilled and plates replenished with further slices of beef, the conversation became more animated. Soon it was the turn of Will Ashley to explain his business.

'I runs my own business 'ereabouts,' he said with a flourish. 'I've a dray and two 'osses stabled off Tooley Street. Every day I goes out into the city loaded up with anything you please, and tek 'em to where as they're wanted. I reckon I knows every inch of the city, but I even goes further. I might tek a load out of town, so to speak, to the villages out west such as Pimlico or Kensington, or north to Islington and Camden Town.'

Mary absorbed this information with interest, and was able to interrupt Will's flow of words when he paused to drink some ale.

'We've come to London to seek work,' she said. 'Do you know of any position open here for Adam?'

'What can you do?' asked Will, pointing a spoon in Adam's direction.

'I work with 'osses,' Adam replied.

'Oh, we don't have your country nags 'ere,' said Will in a jovial fashion. 'This is London, and we work with thoroughbreds here.'

Adam stiffened and was about to rise to Will's bait when he caught sight of Mary's glance of warning. 'I can work with all sorts of 'osses,' he said. ''Ave done so for years, and I can ride as well as any man.'

'Well,' said Will thoughtfully, leaning back in his chair. 'I'm a loner myself – no wish to take on a partner, so to speak, but I did 'ear as that big Ben at the Black Swan was looking for 'elp.'

'Who's big Ben?' Mary and Adam asked, almost simultaneously.

'That's Ben Bickerstaff, the ostler at the Black Swan, off Holborn. He's getting on a bit these days, and like I said, he wants a likely lad to help out.'

'I wonder if I could also find work at this Black Swan place?' Mary queried.

'I shouldn't wonder,' rejoined Will. 'You could try your luck with Nan Butler and see what she can offer.'

'Now, who is Nan Butler?' Mary asked again.

'Why, bless you country folk!' exclaimed Will. 'Why, everybody 'ere knows Jed and Nan Butler runs the Black Swan, and very successful, too. Two years ago Jed landed a wonderful contract, a real money spinner. Three days a week the coach leaves there for York. Black Swan to Black Swan it goes, and three days a week he welcomes it back. A real gem of a business! Yes, Nan Butler's a good sort and might well give you a place with the housekeeping.'

'I'm not having my wife clean out chambers for any Tom, Dick or Harry that comes off of a stagecoach,' Adam retorted sharply.

'Hush, my love,' soothed Mary. 'Remember, we're in this together, and we must both seek work, no matter how hard it may seem at first.'

Mary put her hand into Adam's and gave it a gentle squeeze, which had the desired effect of calming his sudden outburst.

'You know,' said Will, adopting the air of a good fairy granting a wish. 'You could be lucky. Very lucky indeed.' He paused, and waved his pipe about in sweeping circles through the air, giving added drama to his words.

'At first light tomorrow, I'm loading up with 'enry's sacks of corn, and shall be going down Holborn on m'way to some of the inns out on the west side. I could drop you off near the Black Swan. You'll 'ave to make your own way back, mind.'

Mary did her best to accept Will's offer calmly, but inwardly she felt full of excitement, and scarcely paid any attention to the subsequent banter and chit-chat between Tolly, Will and his aunt on matters of local gossip. At length, Will got up to go and retrieved his hat from on the stairs.

'Eight it is, then, at the door,' said Will. 'I'll be loaded up and ready for off by eight.'

'We'll be ready,' Mary replied firmly.

After Will's departure, Mistress Ashley indicated in an obvious fashion by clearing the table that it was time for all to retire.

'Must get ready for an early start on the morrow,' she said, feigning a stifled yawn. 'A good night to you both.'

Mary and Adam gave thanks to their hostess, and after returning 'good nights' to her and Tolly, they climbed the stairs, walked through the first bedroom and into their own. It was not long before Mary's curiosity about Henry Tolly's arrangements for the night was satisfied. She noticed earlier that Tolly had brought no bag or package from the ship, and having observed the closeness between Tolly and Bessy Ashley throughout the evening, it came as no great surprise to hear sounds of an intimate encounter from the adjoining bedroom.

'Who said a sailor has a girl in every port?' Mary whispered in Adam's ear as they lay in bed together. 'Truly, it has been a day to remember.'

She blew out the candle and moved her body closer to Adam's.

Chapter Ten

As Mary had promised, the couple were ready and waiting outside the door of Mistress Ashley's lodging house by eight the next morning, in good time to see Will and his dray approach from Hay's Wharf. Mary had donned a clean white muslin blouse and her best plaid skirt. On her head she wore a white mobcap, which she hoped would give the impression of experienced domesticity. Adam, for his part, had borrowed an old rag and brush from Mistress Ashley, and done his best to clean his riding boots. It was all that he could do under the circumstances to look the part of a journeyman ostler.

Will hailed the two with a loud greeting, and helped Mary up onto the bench seat at the front of the dray.

'You'll have to make do with the corn for a seat,' said Will airily to Adam. 'Hang on tight, and mind you don't fall off!'

On the journey Will patently enjoyed his new and unexpected role as a cicerone for the newcomers. Turning out of Tooley Street they beheld a high gatehouse, which marked the south entrance to London Bridge. Once through the gateway, they marvelled at the density of traffic, the equal of which they had never seen before in their lives. The narrow highway, sandwiched between houses, was thronged with a bewildering assortment of horses, carriages, carts and pedestrians, all moving from side to side and in opposite directions. Mary and Adam looked on in amazement and marvelled at Will's undoubted skill in guiding his two horses through such an irregular movement of massed humanity and vehicles.

'It gets easier at the north end,' Will cried reassuringly. 'They've widened the road up there after the great fire of 66.'

Having successfully negotiated London Bridge, Will continued onwards, constantly urging the horses to cross from one side of the road to another, to avoid the oncoming throng of traffic. As they entered Cheapside, Mary espied the imposing white building they had seen the previous day from the river.

'That's the new cathedral they're building,' shouted their guide, above the noise and bustle in the street. 'The old church burnt down. They do say as this un's going to have a dome, bigger than the Pope's in Rome. One in the eye for him, I says.'

It took another half-an-hour for Will to reach Holborn. Standing up and pulling hard on the reins, he brought the horses to a halt beside a narrow side street, which led off from the main highway.

'The Black Swan's down there, afore you reach Barnards Inn,' Will called. He assisted Mary down to the ground and Adam climbed down from his perch on the sacks.

'Good luck at the Swan,' continued Will. 'I'll see you at Aunt Bessy's for supper.'

With a cheery wave of his hand, Will slapped the reins on the rumps of the horses, and with a jolt the dray moved off in the direction of Holborn Bar and out of the city. Mary smoothed down her skirt and adjusted the mobcap on her head. After a second's pause, she grasped Adam's hand, and slowly, without a word spoken, they walked together down the side street.

In less than two minutes they arrived outside the Black Swan Inn. The inn was an impressive sight. On the left-hand side, the building rose three storeys high. Covered by a whitewashed stucco, the front was punctuated by neat rows of uniformly-sized latticed windows. A large panelled door provided an entrance by foot, and above the door swung a handsome sign depicting a nesting black swan. On the right hand side was a wide archway and opening, which the visitors correctly surmised would lead to the inn's rear yard and stables. Above the arch, and continuing to the other extremity of the inn, were two upper galleries, projecting out some three or four feet from the wall of the inn into the street.

For a few moments Mary and Adam surveyed the inn from the street in silence. Finally, it was Mary, showing her usual determination, who broke the silence.

'Time to see big Ben!' She forced a laugh, and squeezed Adam's hand. 'You'll need to go through the archway, I fancy, whilst I try my luck with Nan Butler inside.'

'Are you sure this is right?' Adam asked falteringly, his courage suddenly deserting him.

Mary ignored Adam's question. She kissed him and gently propelled him with her arm towards the archway. She watched him walk slowly away, giving her a last glance before moving out of sight.

Satisfied all was well, Mary made her way through the front entrance of the inn. It was not yet ten in the morning, but she was greeted by the sight of waiters in their long white aprons hurrying about carrying trays of food and drink for customers who were sitting in various oak-panelled waiting rooms. One of the waiters directed Mary towards a pantry at the rear, where she found Mistress Nan

Butler. Now used to seeing hostesses of a formidable stature, Mary was surprised to find the lady of the house to be a rather small, neat woman, wearing a simple brown dress which reached down to her ankles. Tied with a large bow at the small of her back was a white apron, which covered her front from chest height down to below her knees.

Nan Butler listened to Mary's request with some curiosity.

'Never been to London before?' she queried. 'What experience of inn work have you had?'

'None,' admitted Mary. 'But I've looked after a large house for many years. I'm not afraid of hard work.'

'I dare say as you're not,' replied the innkeeper cautiously,' but it ain't really the same. Show me your hands.'

Mary held out her hands for inspection.

'More the hands of a lady, I'd say, but I'm sure if needs must they'll turn in an honest day's work. I've just lost a still room girl . . .
,

'I'm an excellent hand at making jams, compotes and pickles,' Mary interrupted eagerly.

'Just so,' continued Nan Butler, 'but you'll be needed to help out where I says -the bedrooms and dining rooms. We've all manner of passengers here using our rooms, waiting for coaches and the like.'

To Mary's intense relief a bargain was struck, and with this assurance of employment, Mary felt bold enough to mention Adam's situation and his desire for a job with the horses.

'Well,' said Nan after a pause. 'If Ben takes on this young husband of yorn, I'll let you have one of the stable boys' rooms above the stable. It's nothing grand, and I'll deduct a few pence for your board and lodging, but I dare say it will keep you both dry,' she concluded with a smile.

Mary went out of a back door and into the yard at the rear of the inn. Overjoyed, she felt her heart thumping wildly with excitement. When she saw Adam standing in the middle of the yard, she instinctively knew all was well, for as one not given to idle smiling, Adam's face beamed broadly at the approaching figure of Mary.

'I start in the morning,' he called. 'Ben's taking me on to see what I can do. I start in the morning just as soon as I can get here from Mistress Ashley's.'

'Dearest,' cried Mary. 'I knew it would all come aright. I too have been taken on. Nan Butler's going to see how I fare about the inn. I'll not let her down, just you see, dearest. And guess what?'

'No idea!' Adam exclaimed happily, intrigued by the mystery.

'She's going to let us have one of the stable boys' rooms, somewhere over there.' Mary pointed excitedly in the direction of an upper corridor leading to rooms over the horse boxes.

'I'm well used to that!' Adam laughed, and threw his arms up in the air in a show of mock resignation.

'I knew we'd be saved,' Mary said triumphantly. 'Now we need never look back. We'll become Londoners!'

Joyfully, they walked out hand-in-hand through the archway and began the long walk back to Mistress Ashley's lodging house.

* * * * *

So it was that Mary and Adam began their new life in the metropolis. A year or two later, the pair had established themselves as important and trusted employees at the Black Swan. Mary became the indispensable aid to Nan Butler and helped her run the domestic arrangements at the inn. Ben Bickerstaff's poor health finally forced him to give up work, and Adam took his place as the inn's ostler, becoming a notable figure with those of the inn-keeping fraternity in and around the west end of the city.

Commensurate with their newly-found status, the pair were no longer obliged to stay in a cramped and noisy room above the stable of the inn. Small but comfortable lodgings in the nearby Gray's Inn road were rented from a friend of the Butlers who was leaving the city for Bristol.

As far as the lovers were concerned, there was no doubt that they had succeeded in making good their escape from Holderness and the scene of their crime. Moreover, they had quickly gained an air of solid respectability in their new surroundings. All appeared to be well, but evil, they say, never prospers.

Chapter Eleven

The village of Patrington could fairly be described as a neat, small market town. Here were no low thatched cottages, typical of so many poor Holderness villages. The road leading into the town was lined on either side by well-built farmhouses and residences; two-storey structures with pleasing red brick walls and red pantile roofs. At a fork in the road, the north side continued this residential scene, which included the Manor House, standing a few feet back from the highway. The southern fork led to the market place, which was well supplied with shops and taverns. Here was the centre of a daily bustle of trade, full of carriers arriving and leaving with waggons loaded with goods and produce. Particularly busy was a side track to the east of the village, which led to the corn mill and a small, but useful, harbour at Patrington Haven. The crowning glory of the village, however, was the church of St Patrick, a medieval masterpiece of white limestone, with its gleaming spire rising majestically over the village and beyond.

By the year 1712 Catherine had spent almost four years living with the Dunn family at the Manor House. For all their recent sadness at the loss of a second parent, the Dunn household was not a sombre place, and there was frequent laughter to be heard about the house. They welcomed Catherine as one of their own, and for her part, Catherine was grateful for the love and affection she received from her young friends. As the weeks and months passed by, she began to feel one of the family and, indeed, helped Anne to bring up the twins, James and Frances. All ideas of their house being a temporary home for Catherine were soon forgotten.

Frequent visitors to the house were the rector, John Pighills, and his wife Phyllis. The couple kept a close eye on the young people, and in many ways acted as their surrogate parents. It became something of a ritual that once a week all would take supper together, either at the Dunns or at the parsonage house. The friendship with the Pighillses was another great source of comfort to Catherine. When the Dunns assisted with various little services at the church, Catherine gladly joined in, feeling only pleasure, instead of the former irksome sense of drudgery which attended similar labours done for her uncle at St Peter's by the sea.

Inevitably there were painful, dark thoughts which troubled Catherine's mind. At table the subject of the disappearance of her uncle was rarely mentioned directly, but Catherine always sensed that those around her had an intense curiosity as to what had taken place.

The terrible events of that June evening at Owthorne haunted her constantly. For her it was an unending moral dilemma; an inner struggle of conscience between a sense of doing right by exposing the truth, against the solemn vow of silence given to her sister. All too clearly she saw that to break her vow would place her sister in mortal danger.

Concerning Mary there was another matter which caused Catherine much unhappiness. Months after moving to the Manor House she received a letter from Mary. Whilst overjoyed to learn that her sister was well and happily settled in London, the letter contained a disappointing lack of information. Worse still, Mary did not include any address to which a reply could be sent. A year later Catherine received a second letter, but to her utter dismay it was couched in the same vague terms. The rector expressed his sympathy, and did his best to reassure Catherine that all must be well with her sister in London. Nevertheless, he too was puzzled at the strange lack of detail in the letters, and this only added to his curiosity concerning the mystery of the Sinclare family.

One factor remained unchanged from the old days at Owthorne. Catherine's health continued to be a cause for concern. Her bouts of violent coughing continued unabated, and caused the rector to insist on calling Mr Leonard Tymm from Hedon to come to the Manor House.

Tymm was a highly respected apothecary, who had built up a flourishing practice among the gentry of Holderness. At John Pighills' request, Tymm rode out to Patrington to examine the patient. On arrival, he tapped and prodded Catherine's front and back. He studiously examined a sample of her urine and stools, but came to no greater conclusion than that there was an inherent weakness of constitution which required the utmost care, with a requirement to maintain a routine of genteel living, with no hint of excitement which could aggravate the symptoms. To alleviate the bouts of coughing, Tymm then turned to physical intervention. With the delicacy of a man well used to treating ladies of superior standing, he warmed a metal cup with spirit and placed it above Catherine's right breast. This had the apothecary's desired effect of blistering the skin, but caused poor Catherine intense pain. This she bore with great fortitude, all the while holding Anne's hand in a vice-like grip for support. The physical procedure was completed by the removal of half a pint of blood from a vein in the patient's left arm, which dripped at a steady pace into a silver bowl positioned below her outstretched arm. Satisfied that all that could be done physically had been done, Tymm concluded by recommending a strong and most efficacious mixture, which he would have his assistant make up at Hedon and ride over with on the following day. On hearing this Catherine groaned inwardly, and her mind went back to the days when she used to walk to Widow Preston's shop and try out her concoctions at a penny a time.

After the second letter from Mary, Catherine received no further communications from London, and as time went by, she learnt not to waste time listening out for the sound of the riding postman who occasionally brought mail to the Manor House. She began to take a philosophical view of her situation, and was content to enjoy the happier moments with the Dunns and Pighillses and to suffer in silence her constant agonies of conscience and her poor health.

From time to time John and Phyllis Pighills would invite the Dunns and Catherine to join them for pleasant carriage rides into Hull, or to visit some mutual friends in Holderness. So it was that one Saturday morning in April, arrangements were made for Anne and Catherine to accompany the Pighillses on an outing to Hedon. The intention was not only to enjoy the first signs of spring along the highway, but also to allow Phyllis and Anne to purchase some produce from the market stalls in the new market place of that small borough. Catherine always enjoyed these outings, and looked forward to the arrival of the rector's chaise at the door of the Manor House. True to form, the smart, open four-seater arrived promptly at eight o'clock that Saturday morning, with the rector's man, John Turner, at the reins. With a beaming smile and a loud 'Good morning, ladies!' the rector alighted from the vehicle and helped the two ladies up into their seats facing each other.

The journey began well. The party was in an animated mood, and the conversation en route flowed freely. This general air of happy well-being was matched by the passing rural scene, with sunshine lighting up the neat rows of green shoots in the cornfields. The White Horse tavern at Ottringham came and went, and it was not until the mill at Keyingham was reached that the four commented that the sun had disappeared behind a thickish black cloud. Then, and to the consternation of the rector's wife, it soon became obvious that they were in danger of being caught in a rain storm.

'My dears,' warned Phyllis, 'I fear we are poorly prepared for April showers. What are we to do, John?'

The rector could only offer the protection of two woollen blankets to supplement the flimsy sun umbrellas carried by the ladies.

'Turner,' the rector called. 'Turn around, please. Let us take shelter at the White Horse. Make haste, man!'

No sooner had the rector given the command than an exceptionally heavy burst of rain followed. By the time Turner had manoeuvred the chaise around and retraced the road back to Ottringham, all in the carriage were well and truly soaked to the skin. At that point it was decided unanimously not to seek shelter at the tavern but to press on back to Patrington, where they could all change out of their wet clothes in more comfort.

Turner forced the horse to maintain a fierce pace, but all the while the rain continued to fall incessantly, hampering their progress. At last, after a drive of ten minutes, the reached the Manor House.

In their sodden state, the scene as Catherine and Anne stepped down from the chaise was one of almost comical proportions, and when John Pighills assisted them down, Catherine could not help but smile that the rainwater spouting from the three open corners of the rector's hat looked like water gushing out from some church gargoyle.

'Dear Catherine and Anne,' called a concerned Phyllis from the chaise. 'Do not delay to remove all your wet clothes and remain by the fire until you are quite recovered. A drop of brandy will not come amiss.'

The two wasted no time in prolonged goodbyes, and once inside the front door they were soon being assisted out of their wet clothes by the two housemaids. Moments later they were both enveloped in bathrobes, and seated in front of a hastily lit fire in the parlour.

For a day or two nothing remarkable occurred. The aborted outing came to be regarded in the house as something of an adventure, and Anne and Catherine were obliged to endure a deal of gentle ribaldry from the younger members of the family, who made mock complaints that the promised delicacies from the Hedon market had been denied to them. By the Monday evening, however, Catherine was forced to admit that she was not feeling well, and retired early to her bed.

Before retiring herself, Anne looked in on Catherine, and was shocked to see that her friend was shaking, and looked to have caught a chill. A worried Anne immediately went to the scullery to prepare a warm drink of milk fortified by a measure of laudanum. Catherine gratefully accepted the drink, and giving firm reassurances that all would be well by the morning, she waved away Anne's suggestion that she should sleep in Catherine's room that night. Sadly, in the morning it was all too clear that Catherine was not better, and without delay Anne sent her brother George round to the parsonage house, with an urgent request for Phyllis Pighills to come to the Manor House instantly.

It was soon apparent to all who stood around Catherine's bed that her condition had worsened. Far from the earlier symptoms of a chill, she was now running a temperature, and her frequent coughing bouts were a great drain on her strength.

'We must send for Mr Tymm at once,' said Phyllis. 'There is not a moment to lose! Speed is of the essence.'

George saddled up as quickly as he could and set off at near-gallop in the direction of Hedon. He reached the home of Leonard Tymm shortly before eleven of the morning, but was downcast to find the apothecary away on business in Hull. Having little choice in the matter, George took his horse to the stables at the Old Sun in St Augustine's gate and spent an anxious three hours pacing the cobbled streets of the borough until Tymm returned from Hull.

Tymm was not pleased at the idea of taking to the saddle yet again after a busy day's work in Hull. Nevertheless, after listening to George's insistent pleadings, he agreed to make the journey to Patrington. Some thirty minutes after George left Hedon, the apothecary set out again, armed not only with his instruments of medicine, but also with a bag of clothes, which would allow him to stay overnight at Patrington.

On arrival at the Manor House, Tymm left his horse with George and went straight upstairs to see Catherine. By this time a fever had taken a strong hold of her, and she had great difficulty in talking. Tymm immediately saw that the situation was ominous, and indeed was probably past the point where his medical skills could be of any assistance.

'I fear I have come too late,' said the apothecary gravely to Anne and Phyllis, who were waiting anxiously downstairs. 'In these cases, the first seven days are critical. If the fever persists after that time, then we cannot save the young lady.'

Anne began to cry, and covered her face with a lace handkerchief. Phyllis Pighills too was without words for a moment, filled with anxiety. At last, regaining some composure, she confronted Tymm.

'Is there nothing we can do for Catherine?' she demanded.

'Little, I fear, but trust in God to ease the fever. We can give a purgative which could carry off the bad humours and bring relief.'

Reaching into his bag, Tymm produced a small bottle of calomel. Giving Phyllis instructions of what to do, he announced that he would stay the night at the Hildyard Arms, from where he could be summoned should there be any change in Catherine's condition.

The next visitor to Catherine's bedside was John Pighills. He felt completely wretched and blamed himself for Catherine's dire situation. Sick at heart, and full of remorse, he harboured self-imposed guilt that he had chosen an open carriage for the outing, thinking only of style and the enjoyment of viewing the countryside. Seeing Catherine's worsening state only served to increase the rector's sense of self-blame, and he sat by the bed, awkward and seemingly unable to help other than to recite prayers. At length he noticed a certain agitation in Catherine's manner, which he could not ascribe to her medical symptoms. He drew his chair closer to Catherine's prone figure, and became aware that she was trying to say something to him.

'Dear Catherine, try to rest. You need to rest,' he said soothingly. But as much as the rector tried to calm Catherine, the more determined she became to gain his attention. With an extreme effort, she managed to make herself audible.

'I must go to Owthorne. I cannot rest until I go there.'

The rector was astonished to hear these words. To his knowledge, over the past three or more years, Catherine had never once shown the slightest hint of a desire to return to her former home. Surely, the rector thought, this request must have some link with the disappearance of his old friend, Henock Sinclare? For all that, the request placed him in a terrible dilemma. On the one hand Catherine obviously had a desperate need to go, and on the other hand he could not see how the journey could be accomplished, given the weakened and frail state of her body.

'I cannot rest in peace until I've gone back to the vicarage,' she repeated, the words coming slowly and deliberately as she held the rector in her gaze, the eyes imploring the man to accede to her wish.

'I understand,' said the rector. 'I'll see to it tomorrow, rest assured. Now you must sleep to conserve your energy for the journey. Go to sleep,' he commanded gently, as he first squeezed and then relinquished hold of her hand. Satisfied that Catherine had closed her eyes, he stood up and quietly left the room to join the others waiting downstairs.

All who heard the rector's report of the conversation were amazed at Catherine's demand, and declared unanimously that such a journey would be foolhardy in the extreme, and would inevitably have fatal consequences. The rector agreed, but asked what other choice was possible when the poor girl lying in the bed above was so close to death. And how could they, the rector argued, allow her to meet her Maker with some dark knowledge, or sin un-exorcised, denying her final forgiveness and peace of mind?

In the face of such a powerful argument, they all reluctantly concurred that the journey should take place. It was decided that early the next morning George would ride out to Owthorne to alert John Jordan of the visit and to ensure that the vicarage was open and ready for any purpose that Catherine might require. The Pighills would follow, bringing Catherine in a closed carriage, to reach the vicarage by mid-morning. Exhausted and in low spirits, the couple bade goodnight to the Dunns and left the Manor House. On their way back to the parsonage house, the rector called in at the Hildyard Arms to inform Tymm of their plans for the morrow. As John Pighills imagined, Tymm was appalled to hear of the plan and told the rector so in no uncertain terms.

'Are you out of your mind, sir?' Tymm demanded incredulously, quite unable to comprehend any reason for the rector's plan. 'Even to remove that young lady from her bed, let alone undertake some journey in a carriage, will surely be fatal. It just cannot be contemplated!'

'I fear we are caught in a dreadful dilemma,' the rector replied. 'No doubt you are well acquainted with the strange disappearance of my friend Henock Sinclare some years back. We feel sure that poor Catherine needs to return to her old home for some strange reason connected with that event. She is insisting on going even though she must know that the consequences could be fatal.'

Tymm drew himself up to his full height, his face now flushed with professional indignation.

'This is madness, sir.' Tymm almost shouted his words. 'It goes against all known physic. I cannot sanction it and forbid you to take the lady from her bed!'

John Pighills gave a deep sigh. His hands stretched forward as if to plead for sign of support or understanding.

'I've promised Catherine that we will carry out her wishes tomorrow.'

If the rector held out any hope for a medical dispensation, such feelings were instantly dashed.

'It is clear, I can be of no further service here,' Tymm replied. 'Be assured, I hold you entirely responsible for the certain fate of that young lady. I shall return immediately to Hedon, and shall send you my account in due course. Good day, sir!'

Tymm turned on his heels and marched up the stairs of the inn, leaving Pighills alone and dejected. Deep in thought, he trudged back to the rectory, where his anxious wife was waiting.

'My dear,' Phyllis began. 'We must do what Catherine wishes us to do. We have no choice in the matter, and with God's help all may yet be well. Take heart, my dear.'

Consoled by warm words of support from his wife, the rector rallied from his state of despondency and made the necessary arrangements with John Turner for the following day.

Chapter Twelve

On arrival at Owthorne the next morning George had little difficulty finding John Jordan working in the small field near the vicarage. Jordan was now working alone, as Will Fallowdown had left to farm his own strips of land in the open fields of Owthorne, one of several new tenants of Lord Dunbar. The vicarage looked neglected, empty and firmly shut, as the new vicar preferred the comfort of his house at Burstwick to living in this isolated place. Jordan unlocked the door of the house, although he muttered that he could see no point in opening the building.

'There ain't nothing there inside,' he explained. 'Since the robbery, Mr David Sinclare has removed all the furniture and what was of value to Kilham. At least the stables are still in good fettle,' he added with a shrug of the shoulders.

Thankful only that he had found Jordan so easily, George tied his horse to the yard pump and set about to wait for the coach from Patrington. As he did so, he became aware of a steadily growing number of onlookers standing nearby. By the time the Pighillses' coach arrived, some twenty to twenty-five villagers had gathered at the yard gates, all eager to see what would happen. John Pighills looked at the bystanders with some disdain. 'Have they nothing better to do but gawp and gossip like old women,' he muttered under his breath.

To the relief of Phyllis Pighills, Catherine had managed the journey with amazing fortitude, using every ounce of her remaining strength to achieve the feat. She slowly descended from the coach, helped on either side by the rector and his wife. To their surprise she motioned with a hand in the direction of George's tethered horse.

'Catherine wants to mount George's horse!' Phyllis exclaimed in amazement.

'George had better hold her securely, then,' replied her husband. With some difficulty John Pighills and Jordan managed to lift Catherine up into the saddle, where she was held firmly from behind by George. A nod from Catherine gave George the command to walk the horse across the yard. At first, the path taken was over the middle of the open area, and on reaching the stables at the far side, Catherine appeared agitated, and motioned to George to repeat the walk, this time closer to the wall of the vicarage. George obeyed her silent demands, and when near to the building he and the onlookers saw Catherine remove one of her gloves and drop it on the ground. An audible gasp came from the onlookers.

'A sign! My God, a sign!' cried out a voice in the crowd, which had now abandoned all pretence of showing discretion and had advanced well into the yard. Catherine's frail body slumped back against George's chest. It was clear to all who watched that whatever her mission had been at this place, she had accomplished it, albeit in a most dramatic and enigmatic way. At a shouted bidding from the rector, Jordan and Turner rushed forward and lowered Catherine from the saddle. As gently as they could, the exhausted and semi-conscious female was carried to the coach and into the arms of the waiting Phyllis. Without waiting to hear further orders from his master, Turner leapt up onto the box, grasped the reins and aimed the coach through the yard gates, scattering a few bystanders on the way as he set out post-haste back to Patrington.

There was little doubt in John Pighills's mind that Catherine, by dropping her glove, was giving some clue associated with the mystery of the missing vicar, but at that moment he could not fathom what it might be. The next step, however, was obvious, and he quickly called on Jordan to bring spades and a pick. There was no shortage of volunteers for the task, but Jordan pushed aside one or two of those who came forward to volunteer and handed spades to Obediah Kemp and Samuel Owbridge.

'I'll loosen the gravel wi' m' pick, and then you'll find it easy to clear the earth away below,' Jordan commanded, beginning to strike at the compacted surface of the yard.

For some time spadefuls of clay and soil continued to pile up on the side without revealing anything of significance. The onlookers, who had now formed a close circle around the three sweating men, began to be restive and the volume of noise from their idle tongues, each offering some new interpretation on the situation, grew louder. Almost at a point when Kemp thought of taking a breather, his attempt to raise a spadeful of earth met with resistance. Carefully, he scraped away a few clumps of clay and soil and gave a short cry of discovery. Stepping back, he looked at the rector with an air of triumph.'

'No doubtin' it, sir. There's a shoe down there, right enough.'

John Pighills fell to his knees beside the shallow pit. Taking the spade from Kemp's hand, he pulled more earth away from an exposed foot. Jordan began to work in parallel with the rector, and as two legs and thighs were revealed, nobody present could doubt that they had found the body of their missing vicar. It was Jordan who exposed the final portion; a gruesome object, the cloven skull of the missing man, and, even after that length of time buried under the soil, some mangled remains of his brains could still be recognised. One or two of the women in the crowd screamed at the sight; others covered their eyes with their aprons. Seeing their distress, most of the men led their womenfolk away from the scene and back to their cottages. It was a day that no person present would ever forget.

John Pighills was aghast at the sight of his old friend. He looked at Jordan and Kemp, and slowly got to his feet, leaning heavily on the spade for support.

'God reveals all in time, but in strange and mysterious ways,' he said slowly. 'We have found out the truth at last. Poor Mr Sinclare has been foully put to death, and I'm sure we all know who the villain is.'

'No doubt about it, sir,' Jordan replied. 'An' I'd swear to it on the Holy Bible.'

'You may well have to,' said the rector gravely. 'I need to see Mr Waterland immediately to tell him of our terrible discovery. Can I rely on you gentlemen to obtain a stout coffin and place Mr Sinclare safely in it, until I am at liberty to give the poor man a proper and holy burial?'

'Rest assured, Mr Pighills, we'll see to that,' said Jordan. 'But we recommends speed, if you sees our meaning,' he added, giving a purposeful glance in the direction of the badly decomposed corpse.

'There'll be no delay,' the rector replied. 'Make sure the coffin is safely locked away inside the vicarage. Now, if you please, I'd be obliged if you could lend me a horse, so I can return quickly to Patrington. Turner will return with the animal in the morning.'

Jordan saddled up a mare in the stables, and led her out into the yard. With hurried and sombre farewells, the rector and George left Owthorne to make the short journey back to Patrington.

The coach containing the two women had already reached the Manor House about an hour earlier. On arrival Catherine, supported on each side by Phyllis and Anne, had managed to walk from the coach and climb the stairs to her bedchamber without mishap. Propped up by feather pillows, Catherine took a glass of warm milk, softened by a soothing draught of laudanum. To the surprise of the ladies around the bed, Catherine appeared to be no worse for her dramatic excursion. In fact, she exhibited more animation than she had shown since the day before she fell ill. Even her speech, although low in volume and slow in delivery, was perfectly audible and coherent. She apologised for all the trouble she had caused and thanked everyone for their love and tender care. At last, she said she felt tired, and begged to be left alone to sleep a while. When Anne returned to the bedchamber at nine o'clock that evening, she found Catherine still in an upright position, motionless and with her eyes closed. Anne swore to all later that there was a look of serenity on her face. Catherine had died, but, without doubt had left this world at peace with herself and her Maker.

Chapter Thirteen

The courthouse at Burstwick was an ancient structure, half-timbered and covered by a red-tiled roof, which distinguished it from the surrounding thatched cottages of the village. It was here that the lord of the manor held his biannual Great Courts for the freeholders and copyholders of the manor. As far as the oldest people in the village could remember, the building had always stood on this spot and they knew of no other.

Henry Waterland's clerk, Sam Wright, had been busy over the previous days making all the necessary arrangements for the inquest. He had, with no little difficulty, arranged for Leonard Tymm to go to Owthorne vicarage to view the corpse, and had secured his presence today as the first witness. Other witnesses included the Reverends Prowde and Pighills, John Jordan, Obediah Kemp and young George Dunn. Finally, Wright had managed, by dint of travelling from farm to farm, to summon twelve 'good, true and disinterested freeholders' to serve on the jury.

Arriving early that Thursday morning, Wright stabled his horse at the Hare and Hounds and walked across the road to open up the courtroom. Being a sunny April morning, there seemed to be no real need of a fire, but Wright felt a dampness in the air, and as Waterland frequently complained of cold draughts permeating throughout the old building, he set to and lit the stove situated in the centre of the room. One by one he ticked off from his list the names of the witnesses and jury members as they arrived at the courthouse. To Wright's great relief, all those he had summoned were present by the time his principal arrived to take charge of the proceedings. In a loud voice Wright announced the formal opening of the inquest in the name of Her Gracious Majesty, Queen Anne, that twentieth day of April 1712. He then went through the laborious process of swearing in each of the jury members. This formality completed, Wright gave a stiff bow to Waterland, and sat down ready to take notes of the proceedings.

Henry Waterland called the witnesses one by one to take the stand. As each came forward and gave his evidence, it was as if pieces of a jigsaw were being put into place, revealing the full picture of the tragedy. John Jordan and Obediah Kemp each swore that the body they had uncovered was that of their missing vicar, the Reverend Henock Sinclare. Leonard Tymm affirmed the cause of death as being from a blow to the head by a sharp instrument, and stated that in his opinion the state of the body corresponded to the time that the vicar had gone missing. Next up on the stand was the Reverend Samuel Prowde. He spoke of his conversation with Mary Sinclare, when she told him of her intention to marry Adam Alvin. He went on to describe the secret preparations made for the wedding at Halsham. John Pighills gave more information regarding the behaviour of the couple, and what he knew of Henock Sinclare's opposition to their marriage. Adding to this, Henry Waterland himself was able to relate the gist of his own interview with Adam, when the servant had told him of his intention to marry Mary Sinclare.

With the evidence of all these witnesses having been heard by the jury and recorded by Wright, Waterland felt satisfied that the jury had enough facts on which to reach a verdict, and asked them to withdraw to the adjoining small chamber to consider the case. In the event, there was little surprise at seeing the jury file back into the courtroom after an interval of only some fifteen minutes.

'Have you reached your verdict?' Waterland asked the foreman of the jury.

'We have, sir.'

'And are you unanimous in your verdict?'

'We are, sir.'

'Then please tell the court.'

'We find that the Reverend Henock Sinclare has been foully done to death and has been murdered by his man-servant, Adam Alvin.'

John Pighills was wholly expecting the given verdict, but was rather taken by surprise when Waterland further questioned the foreman.

'Thank you,' Waterland said. 'Is that the full extent of your verdict? Have you nothing further to add?'

'No, sir. That is all we do say and have agreed.'

'Then, thank you again, gentlemen. You are all discharged and may go.'

Leaving Wright to tidy up his papers and close the courtroom, Waterland and the rector walked over to the Hare and Hounds to take a glass of brandy together. John Pighills was curious to learn what had prompted the Hedon lawyer to quiz the foreman of the jury as to their verdict, one which the rector believed was entirely proper and satisfactory.

'Well,' Waterland began. 'I say this from a cold point of law, you understand. The jury, and no doubt rightly, find Alvin guilty of committing this crime, but what about Mary and her possible part in this affair? She could have been an accomplice in the crime. The motive is quite clear.'

'Surely not,' Pighills replied in astonishment. 'I've known the two young ladies, living with Henock, for nigh on ten years. Mary and Catherine could never be accused of such a terrible crime. You know that poor Catherine has now departed this life?'

'Indeed,' Waterland continued. 'Amen to that, but before death she revealed the place where poor Sinclare was buried, so she must have known about the murder. And if she knew, then Mary must have known also. No doubt at all she stood to benefit from her uncle's removal, as 'tis well-known he opposed her marriage to that good-for-nothing.'

John Pighills sighed. He could see the logic in the case Waterland was putting forward, although it went against his nature ever to think of accusing Mary Sinclare, or even Catherine, of involvement in the crime.

'I understand,' said the rector at last. 'I fear though that we may never get to the truth of the matter. Catherine has died, God rest her soul, and the other two birds have flown the nest. We have no notion of where they may have settled in the great City of London.'

'I fear you may be right,' said Waterland. 'But I feel bound to advise the Sheriff to issue a warrant for the arrest of both of them. We've done all we can in this place, but I must also inform David Sinclare at Kilham. No doubt the verdict will be of some great relief, as it will at last allow him to settle the estate of his brother.'

* * * * *

At seven o'clock of a September evening, daylight was still in evidence as the horses of the York coach clattered under the archway and into the yard of the Black Swan at Holborn. What had previously been a scene of relative calmness and quiet erupted into a frenzy of activity and noise. The coachman, resplendent in a huge overcoat of brown worsted cloth and tricorn hat coloured to match, stood up bellowing a command, 'Whoa!' and pulled back the reins with all his might. The coach now stationary, his assistant immediately leapt down from the box and began to help the outside passengers down from the rear seats of the coach. From the door of the inn appeared a number of porters, who ran to the coach and began to unbuckle the boxes and hampers strapped to the roof of the vehicle. Having safely assisted the outside passengers down, the assistant coachman turned his attention to helping out the inside passengers. Having placed a wooden step in front of the door, he offered his arm to the emerging ladies, and smoothly accepted the proffered tips from the gentlemen with a smart touch of the hat. Slowly, all the passengers disembarked, and following two ladies out of the coach, the Reverend John Pighills was pleased to feel solid ground again beneath his feet. He stretched his cramped limbs and looked about him, happy to spot his wooden boxes, which contained his clothes and papers, disappearing into the inn, carried by porters.

It had not been a bad journey, an uneventful ride from York in what was generally acknowledged to be an excellent month in which to travel, with no snow, ice or strong winds to contend with. He rarely came to London, but on this occasion, as Dean of South Holderness, he was obliged to attend an ecclesiastical meeting at Lambeth Palace on the following day. For the night, he had reserved a chamber at the Black Swan, an arrangement for which he had little enthusiasm, as it would mean using a fourth bed in as many nights. It had not helped either that he had been obliged to pay what he considered an exorbitant price for the privilege of not having to share his bed with any fellow travellers.

Guided by the ever-attentive assistant coachman, John Pighills and the other passengers shuffled across the yard in the direction of the door leading into the inn. As he was about to enter, he glanced to his left and noticed their coachman in conversation with another man. The rector stopped, as if dead in his tracks. Surely he knew this second man? The face seemed familiar, but how could it be, as he knew not a soul in those parts, so far from his usual surroundings. Determined to satisfy his curiosity, Pighills moved up to the assistant coachman, and pointing discreetly in the direction of the two men, enquired who it was talking to their driver.

'That, sir, is Mr Alvin, the ostler of this inn.'

Pighills gave a short gasp of astonishment, and then doing his utmost to adopt a casual, more matter of fact air to cover his excitement, he continued, 'Would that be Mr Adam Alvin, I suppose?'

'Yes, indeed,' said the coachman, and waited with an expectant smile as the reverend produced another gratuity from a coat-tail pocket.

'Thank you kindly, sir. Have a very good stay in London, an' we'll be pleased to see you safely back to York when it's convenient, sir.'

The rector followed a porter up two flights of stairs and into a small upper chamber with windows overlooking the street below. He took advantage of the porter's presence to order some supper and ale, requesting that it be brought up to his room. He then sat down to wait for his boxes to arrive. On their receipt, and the porter having obtained the customary tip, the rector felt it prudent to confirm his discovery, so there could be no possible mistake on a matter of such gravity. In the course of questioning the porter, it soon became apparent that there was no mistake. In addition, he learnt that the ostler and his wife, described by the porter as the inn's assistant housekeeper, had arrived at the inn from Yorkshire some four years previously.

The rector pondered for some time on the quickest way he might send word to Henry Waterland, to tell him of his amazing and fortuitous discovery. It would, at best, be another five days before he returned to Holderness, but against this he had little faith in the General Post Office delivering a letter in less time. At last he plumped for a letter, and drawing out a sheet of paper, a quill and a small bottle of black ink from one of his boxes, he wrote detailing the circumstances of finding the wanted couple at the inn. Folding the paper carefully, he addressed the front, lit a candle beside his bed, warmed a stick of wax, and sealed the fold of the paper using his signet ring. Satisfied with his work, the rector pulled the bell tug and awaited the arrival of a porter. Within a minute or two a thin, lanky lad of about thirteen years of age, with a pock-marked face and mop of reddish hair, appeared at the door.

'I require this letter to go immediately to the General Post,' the rector commanded.

'It'll go first thing in the morning,' said the lad with an audible sniff of the nose. 'Single sheet, is it? Like as not, I'll be the one taking it to our local receiving house, Mr Place, the stationer at Gray's Inn Gate. 'Course, there's a charge of a penny to 'im to deliver it to the General an' all, sir. But I'll do it first thing,' the lad added pointedly.

Pighills groaned inwardly. London, he feared, would prove to be a very expensive place. He handed over a silver threepenny coin, and waved away the lad's pretence of looking for change.

'How long will it take to get to Yorkshire?' asked the rector.

'About three days, sir. That's if the post boys don't fall asleep on their 'orses,' he added with a laugh. 'Thank you kindly, sir. Will that be all you're needing for now, sir?'

Determined to get value for his coin, Pighills sat down on a chair. 'I'd be obliged if you'd help me off with my boots' he said, and before the lad could make any reply, he thrust out a leg in the lad's direction.

The rector retired to bed soon after eating his supper. He slept well, enjoying a warm feeling of contentment, sure that he had done his duty by his old friend Henock Sinclare.

* * * * *

In spite of John Pighills's plea for urgency, almost a month passed before two men walked into the Black Swan Inn, one carrying a large leather bag. Jed Butler instantly recognised the men as the parish constables from the Watch House, near Holborn Barrs, the local 'lock-up'.

'Come to take my good woman away, 'ave you?' he said jokingly to the pair.

'No, Jed,' replied the first. 'But you're not far from the mark. We want your ostler and 'is missus.'

Jed's face lost its jovial appearance. In an instant his expression changed to one of surprise and amazement.

'There must be some mistake. Adam and Mary are first-rate people. They've been with me these past four years. Part of the family, so to speak. They're as honest as the day's long.'

'No mistake, I'm afraid,' returned the first constable. 'We've a warrant here for both of 'em. It's a felony of a serious kind. Summat from years back, up north, I fancy.'

'Well, I'll let Adam put you right himself,' said Jed, and turning round, he gave a passing porter an order to fetch the ostler.

Adam came into the inn, annoyed at being disturbed from a task of dealing with an injured horse that had been left by a traveller. Recognising the two constables with Jed, however, quickly put him on his guard. Approaching the group, he also noted the look of concern on the face of the innkeeper.

'You wanted to see me,' said Adam gruffly. 'I don't want to tarry, I'm busy with a sick 'orse.'

Jed did not reply, but merely nodded his head in the direction of the first constable.

'Adam Alvin, I've a warrant for your arrest on a charge of murder. You'll have to come with us, but we needs take Mistress Alvin on a similar charge.'

Adam was stunned by the words of the constable. He looked about him wildly, as if contemplating some means of escape, but as he did so, the second constable stepped forward, opened the leather bag, and grasping Adam's arm began to secure iron shackles on his wrists.

'I don't know what you're talking about,' Adam cried. 'I've done nothing. Nothing at all!' He looked in desperation at Jed, who looked equally shocked at what was happening to his ostler.

When Mary was called to the scene, she needed only a second's glance at the anguished face of her husband and the sight of the shackles about his wrists, to give a loud scream and fall in a fainting fit upon the floor. Nan Butler, who had followed Mary into the room, rushed to her aid and water was brought to revive the prone woman. Once conscious and seated on a chair, Mary received the same dreadful bidding from one of the constables, and in spite of loud protests from Nan and Jed, she, too, was put in shackles. After a few heated words were exchanged between Jed and the constables, the pair were bundled into a closed carriage and taken on a short journey to the Watch House. As the heavy door of the cell closed behind them, and they heard the key turn in the lock, Mary burst into floods of tears. She clung to Adam in the semi-darkness of their confined space, and it seemed an eternity before they were able to take stock of their new situation.

The cell was square in shape, with walls of stone. These stones had probably once been white in colour, but had now blackened with age and neglect. Aided by a constant dampness, green moss flourished in the corners of the cell. One small barred window was positioned high up on a south-facing wall, which permitted some light into the space below. Opposite was the entrance door, of stout construction, the upper part open but heavily barred, giving a view of the adjoining room where the constables were stationed. A broad wooden bench and a cracked chamber pot completed the furniture in the cell, except for some handfuls of dirty-looking straw strewn about the floor, which gave off an unpleasant and unmistakeable odour of urine.

As usual, it was Mary who was the first to recover some sense of rational thought, and brushing aside her tears, she did her best to comfort her distraught husband.

'This cannot be right,' she said. 'There must be some mistake. How could anyone discover any evidence against us?'

There was a moment's pause for thought, then Adam replied in a low voice, 'Your sister must 'ave blabbed. It can only be 'er what's done this.'

'Never! Never would Catherine betray us. She swore on the bible she would never tell a living soul. She wouldn't break that vow, I'm certain of it.'

'What's going to happen now?' Adam asked.

'I don't know, sweetheart, but we must be strong and deny any charges put to us. There can be no case against us.'

To the couple's great relief, an hour or so after their arrival at the Watch House Nan Butler appeared at the cell door, carrying some clothes for Mary and a little money. It was a great comfort to Mary to see Nan, and although they could not embrace, they were able to hold hands through the bars of the door and converse, albeit under the watchful eye of a constable.

'Do you know what's going to happen to us?' Mary asked Nan.

'The constables tell me you'll both go before the magistrates later this afternoon. They think you'll be sent back to Yorkshire.'

Mary groaned in despair at the thought of returning north. It felt as if she had enjoyed some wonderful dream, only to awake and find reality a living nightmare from which there was no escape. Nevertheless, the pair were pitifully grateful to Nan for her visit, and before she left the Watch House she promised to prepare some plates of cold meat and pickles to fortify them for the ordeal ahead. To secure this promise, Nan was obliged to part with more of her money to one of the jailors, to persuade him to fetch the food over from the Black Swan.

As Nan had predicted, around two o'clock in the afternoon Mary and Adam were led out from their cell and taken by the constables' coach a short distance of some two hundred yards to the rear of Furnival's Inn. The inn was Holborn's largest tavern, and it served a dual function. Not only did it stand as a traditional hostelry, but it also acted as the local courthouse. After waiting in a dark corridor for some time, Mary and Adam were ushered into the courtroom and motioned to stand side by side inside a boxed enclosure in the centre of the room. Above them, on a raised platform, were seated three justices of the peace, and directly below the bench sat the clerk, complete with large tome open on his desk and quill pen poised in his right hand. There seemed to be a number of other men seated in various places around the room, but the couple's attention was firmly concentrated on the faces of the three men on the bench. Mary and Adam's worst fears were soon to be realised.

The session began with the clerk formally establishing their identity. He then proceeded to read out the charges. They were both short and succinct. Adam and Mary were charged with the act and complicity in the wilful murder of one, Henock Sinclare, on the 10th day of June in the year of Our Lord 1708, in the parish of Owthorne, in the East Riding of Yorkshire. Attention then turned to the central figure sitting amongst the justices. 'How do you plead to these charges?' he asked Adam and Mary in turn.

By this time both had regained some of their lost composure, and each was able to give a firm reply of 'Not guilty'. They then watched closely as the three men conferred amongst themselves in whispered tones. It mattered little that they could not be overheard, as the central figure of the justices quickly brought the proceedings to an end.

'We order that the prisoners, Adam and Mary Alvin, being charged with a felony, must stand trial at the appropriate assizes. In this case to take place at York Castle. Constables, take the prisoners away and do your duty!'

Alone again in their gloomy cell at the Watch House, Mary and Adam clung to each other for comfort.

'Summat's 'appened back at the village,' Adam said at last. 'They must 'ave dug up the old man. But 'ow did they find us at the Black Swan?'

'I don't know,' Mary replied. 'They can't have discovered Uncle Henock – he was too well hidden – and I'm sure Catherine would never betray us.'

'Then why are we sittin' 'ere?' Adam asked in a miserable tone of voice.

'I don't know,' Mary repeated. 'But whatever happens, we must deny any charges put to us. They cannot prove we are guilty. If we keep to the story that he went over the cliff, we'll be safe. That we married and came to London is not a crime, whatever the villagers of Owthorne may say.'

The pair lapsed into silence, and were content to hold each other as best they could, hindered as they were by their shackles. Little did they know at that moment what had transpired in the vicarage yard far away, nor even that Mary's sister was dead.

That evening Nan and Jed Butler appeared together at the Watch House. Nan brought more food and Jed handed over more money, which he insisted they had a right to take in owed wages.

'I 'ear as you're going up to York,' said Jed. 'This'll come in 'andy when you're there. Sure enough it'll buy a few favours up north, jus' as it do 'ere.' He gave a knowing glance over his shoulder at a constable who was sitting at a nearby table. 'He tells me you're off early int' morning up the Great North Road. I trust all will be well with you both and we'll see you back at the Black Swan ere long, never fear!'

Farewells were painful. Jed did his best to show a manly attitude, called out loudly, 'Good luck to you both,' and turned to leave. Mary's early determination to put on a brave face dissolved rapidly, and through tears she clutched Nan's hands through the cell bars, her 'goodbyes' being scarcely coherent. Nan, too, cried, and finally, overcome with emotion, she fled from the scene to be helped back to the Black Swan on the arm of her husband.

Chapter Fourteen

If the voyage in the Billy Boy to London had been a delight, the return journey to Yorkshire seemed unending torture. The mechanics of travel were simple enough. The prisoners were conveyed in a variety of vehicles, ranging from closed coaches with barred windows, to open wains, by a series of parish constables. At the boundary of every parish they were handed over to the next pair of constables to continue on their journey north. Progress was at a snail's pace, and at nightfall the pair were lodged in the nearest parish lock-up.

Open wains were the worst, for with Mary and Adam fettered hands and legs and unable to move, they were exposed to the elements. Passing through the towns of Huntingdon and Stamford, their plight was only too obvious, and they were subjected to jeers, catcalls and volleys of clods of earth or stones thrown by local urchins who ran behind the wain. Only when one of the constables leapt from his seat and chased them away did the humiliation cease. Comfort at night was nothing but a lottery of chance. In some of the more isolated country villages, a kindly constable's wife might provide them with food, ale and some clean straw to lie on, always, of course, after negotiating with Mary for a suitable payment. In towns on the road, Adam was obliged to share a cell with a number of thieves and ruffians in terrible conditions. Mercifully, Mary was usually lodged alone in some nearby cell. Without exception, no place on the journey provided even the smallest scrap of comfort, but that it had to be bought from their gaolers. As Adam bitterly remarked to Mary, if they had gone to London to be gaolers instead of working in a tavern, they would now be wealthy people.

After two weeks on the road, their last conveyance passed through the village of Riccall, and in the distance could be seen the high towers of York Minster. To Mary and Adam's surprise, the two constables were amiable fellows, and kept up a lively conversation as they approached the city. Turning the horses to the left, the driver steered the wain around the walls of the castle, and rounding the elevated mound of Clifford's Tower on their right hand side, they entered the castle by the North Gate.

'You're in luck,' said one of the constables brightly, as if addressing two newly-arrived guests at a hostelry. 'Not ten year old. A bran' new gaol for you. How does that take your fancy?'

Mary and Adam could think of many, many other places

where they would rather be, and they were not at all comforted by the sight of the newly-built gaol-house on the far side of the castle bailey. They saw, however, that it was a long rectangular structure, with two wings projecting forward at each end, thus providing for an open central courtyard. Above the middle bay was a tower of ashlar stones, flanked by carved scrolls, and above the tower rose a cupola, crowned by a lead-covered dome complete with ball finial and weathervane.

For all the new gaol's splendour, Mary and Adam were in no mood or condition to appreciate the architectural features of the building. Arriving at the courtyard, the constables helped the prisoners down from the wain and escorted them through the main doors of the gaol and into a large entrance hall. Mary and Adam were obliged to shuffle forward rather than walk, because of their heavy leg irons. For all the world to see, they presented as two thoroughly wretched, dirty and bedraggled figures reduced to their lowest level.

The new arrivals were met in the hall by two men. In appearance they could not have been more dissimilar. The first man was tall and almost slender of form. His lean face had a pallid tone and his chin was slightly covered with greyish stubble. His rough and dirty hands seemed to be in keeping with the coarse quality of his old stained coat and breeches, all of which signalled to Mary a person of low station, who might not hesitate to use force on any prisoner not obeying orders. The second man was short and squat of stature, with a round face and ruddy complexion. He wore a long woollen coat and matching brown hat of a style which, whilst old and worn, suggested a taste of former quality. Both men wore a broad leather belt, from which hung a chain, an iron circle and a number of large keys.

One of the accompanying constables doffed his hat to the small squat man. 'Mr Chippendale, sir.' The constable addressed the gaoler in an official-sounding manner. 'We 'ave to deliver these prisoners, Adam and Mary Alvin on a warrant from the 'olborn magistrates. I trust you'll find this 'ere warrant to be in order, sir.'

Mary and Adam watched intently as the constable brought forth from his coat pocket some sheets of paper, and handed them to the gaoler. Without saying a word, the gaoler gave them a cursory glance as he walked over to a small desk in the corner of the hall. There he scratched out a signature on one of the pieces of paper, before returning it to the constable.

'All in order,' the gaoler said abruptly, then added in a menacing tone, 'I don't think we'll have any trouble from these two. You are dismissed!'

'Thank you, sir, and good day to you all.'

The two constables, with almost simultaneous movements, touched their hats in salute, and departed from the scene through the open doors of the hall.

The tall gaoler moved across the hall, unlocked a side door, and motioned to Mary and Adam to enter another room. Once all were inside, the man locked the door behind them.

'Welcome to York Castle,' said the small squat man, and gave a bow larded with more than a touch of sarcasm. 'My name is Edmund Chippendale. I'm the chief gaoler of the castle, and this is Tom, my assistant. Me and Tom will be looking after you both during your stay. It's a good month 'til the next assizes, so you'd better make the best of things. We don't want no trouble, do we?'

Mary and Adam managed the barest of nods. The thought of being in the care of Mr Chippendale and Tom for a whole month filled them both with dread and despair.

'You any friends in York?' enquired Chippendale. ''Ave you?' he repeated loudly after a pause. 'Lost your tongues?'

Mary cleared her throat, and calling on her reserves of courage, she faced her gaoler.

'Mr Chippendale, we have no friends here in York, but I do have a sister in Holderness. I should be obliged if I could write to her for help. Can I have paper, ink and a pen, please?'

'I dare say as 'em could be provided,' Chippendale said. 'We always try to oblige,' he added, with a thin smile. 'Although we shouldn't, you know. But for a little accommodation, it's wonderful what can be done. Really, it is.' He gave another smile, and in turn gave a knowing nod to Mary, followed by an obvious wink of the eye to his assistant.

'Can our chains be removed?' Mary asked.

'Just as soon as we get you into your cell, my dear. An' I'll fetch my good lady to come and see to you when you're settled in, so to speak. This gaol's the newest and best in all England.'

The procedure of unlocking and locking doors behind continued as they moved down a long corridor. Cells on either side soon became apparent by a series of stout wooden doors, each studded with rows of black iron rivets, and furnished with two large sliding bolts, one above and one below, firmly shut and secured by padlocks. A rectangular opening in the top section of every door had superimposed upon it a criss-cross of flat iron bars, leaving only a small aperture through which light could pass and one could see and converse with a prisoner inside.

As the party slowly progressed the noise of their conversation, and the clanking sounds of chains being dragged along the stone flags, instantly sparked off the curiosity of those incarcerated within the cells. The watching eyes of the inmates, visible through the small aperture in each door, soon became apparent to the new arrivals and added to their mounting discomfort.

Mary was the first to reach a vacant cell. Chippendale selected a key and opened the door. At that point, she saw that Tom continued to escort Adam along the corridor.

'Can we not be together?' she cried in anguish. 'We're married!'

'Not allowed, I'm afraid,' replied Chippendale impassively. 'In you go,' he commanded, and pushed Mary into the cell with a not too gentle thrust of his hand on her shoulder.

Adam cried out at the sight of Mary's treatment, but his gaoler was unmoved, and relentlessly guided his prisoner to another cell at the furthest end of the corridor. Chippendale followed Mary into the cell, and ignoring the tears and pleas from the distraught woman, began to remove her fetters.

'I'll send my good woman in shortly to see you,' he said. 'I take it you've some coins handy?' he added as he moved towards the door, pausing on the threshold. 'There's a charge to pay of three and four-pence each for admission. It's to cover the board and lodgin',' he explained coolly.

Mary stared at the gaoler in amazement. She would have dearly loved to remove the smirk on his face with the flat of her hand, but seeing no option but to pay, she searched around for coins in her purse.

'And I suppose if we're found guilty, there'll be another charge to pay,' she retorted with spirit, as she passed over the money.

'That'll be of a different sort,' replied the gaoler, and with that sinister remark, he left the cell.

Mary, alone in her new surroundings, looked about her. In many ways the cell resembled her last place of confinement at the Watch House; square in shape, a single-barred window high up on one of the walls provided the only source of direct sunlight, and internally the small barred aperture on the door allowed some limited view of passers-by in the corridor. Mary noted with some relief that the grey stone walls looked whiter than at the Watch House, and there was no sign of running water, damp or green mould on the walls or ceiling above.

The main difference here, however, was, oh joy of joys, a broad wooden bench which Mary instantly perceived as serving a dual function of seat and bed. No doubt, she thought, a penny or two could provide some comfort with the luxury of a sheet or blanket, and encouraged by the thought of help from Catherine being only a letter and short distance away, Mary reassured herself that all would be well.

The harsh clicking noise of a key opening the two padlocks on the door heralded the arrival of Mistress Chippendale. She was a small, slight woman, her face dominated by a large hooked nose and generally sharp features which, as Mary was to discover in time, matched her manner. Her blouse and skirt were of a plain cloth, and apart from a black shawl around her shoulders, and a white lace bonnet upon her head, she was devoid of decoration. The obvious feature which distinguished Mistress Chippendale from any other ordinary female about the city of York, was the chain hanging from her waist carrying a large number of keys.

'I've brought your belongings,' she said, placing on the bench the bundle of clothes which Nan had brought to the Watch House. Mary gave her thanks. Distracted by the sequence of events on entering York Castle, she had quite forgotten this small bundle, which now represented her sole belongings of any practical value.

'You want to write a letter, I hear. It'll cost a shilling. Have you got a shilling?' she demanded sharply.

Mary produced the silver coin from a purse which she now kept securely hidden in a pocket sewn inside one of her petticoats, and handed it over. By this time she had grown quite accustomed to the blatant extortion practised by all those connected with the prison system, only comforting herself that this investment would bring her and her husband the means towards a more tolerable existence until they could be cleared of all charges at the assizes.

Mary wrote the letter the next day. She described to Catherine all that had befallen them since their arrest at the Black Swan; their plight at the castle, and begged for aid in sending clothes and money to ease their days in the gaol. Most of all, she begged for a visit from her dear sister. Every minute space on the single sheet of paper provided was filled by Mary's written cry for help.

Chippendale slowly read the letter in front of Mary, who felt mortified at this lack of privacy. Eventually, he lowered the paper, sniffed loudly, and wiped his nose on the sleeve of his coat.

'This'll be sixpence to take it to the post office in Register Square,' he said, and waited for Mary to produce a coin.

'What! Sixpence, just to take a letter to a post house!' Mary was now feeling quite exasperated at the greed of her gaoler. 'It cannot be more than a street or two away!'

Chippendale shrugged his shoulder. 'Please yourself, my good lady', he said, with mock civility. 'York's an expensive place. Now, I'm a busy man. Make up your mind. Do you want the letter sending or no?'

Mary gave a deep sigh and began to search under her skirt for the money.

* * * * *

Mary's letter placed the household of the Manor House at Patrington in a terrible dilemma. The habitual tenderness of Anne's nature was torn between a thorough loathing for Adam, a proscribed villain and murderer, and the compassion she felt at hearing of Mary's plight at York. Brother George, on the other hand, could never free himself from the memory of the ghastly sight of Henock Sinclare's shattered skull, and expressed no sympathy for the couple incarcerated in York Castle. Uncertain of how to proceed, the Dunns turned for advice to their friends the Pighillses.

One week following his chance discovery of the Alvins at the Black Swan, John Pighills had returned to Patrington. On arrival he immediately went to see Henry Waterland, and was gratified to learn that steps were in hand to bring Mary and Adam back to Yorkshire.

'Now we'll see justice done for our old friend,' he exclaimed to Waterland triumphantly.

On being called to the Manor House, John and Phyllis Pighills walked over to join the Dunns, who were all gathered in the parlour. The news of the receipt of Mary's letter, written from York Castle gaol, filled the rector with unconcealed delight. As George read out the contents, he gave periodic grunts of satisfaction.

'You see,' he said at last. 'Villains never prosper. His will be done on earth as it is in Heaven. I'll see the full justice done for Henock.'

'Surely, you do not see dear Mary as being touched with this dreadful crime?' Anne asked. 'She must be innocent.'

'Perhaps so,' replied the rector. But they'll have a fair trial at York. God knows, right will prevail.'

George, who was always a practical sort of lad, asked what was to be done in response to Mary's letter. Anne suggested that she should go to York to see Mary and to break the news of Catherine's death, but before the rector could reply, Phyllis intervened.

'My dears, I believe Anne should not go to that terrible place, but suffice it to write to Mary to tell her that poor Catherine has passed away. I'm sure it is necessary to send her money and some bedding. A few words of Christian comfort will not go amiss. Perhaps clothes as well . . . and a bible,' she added, looking across at her husband.

'Very wise indeed, my dear,' said the rector, 'but I feel I should ride over to Hedon tomorrow to seek some guidance from Henry Waterland. I'll wager he'll be going to York for the assizes.'

There was general agreement to this suggestion, and early the next morning John Pighills rode to Hedon, carrying Mary's letter in his saddlebag. He found Waterland at home, and lost no time in handing the letter over to the lawyer to read.

'Just so,' said Waterland. 'This is a delicate matter, and under the circumstances I think we must offer help to Mary, but it's not for Anne herself to go to the prison. I think I can help by sending Sam to York with a letter from Anne, some money, and any other comforts the Dunns wish to provide. It's better to hand money over in person these days. You cannot trust the gaolers – they're as bad as the criminals they lock up! I need to send word also to my brother Daniel. I'm sure you know he's Chancellor at the Minster, so he can keep an eye on things and let me know well in advance when the trial will take place.'

'Very good of you, Henry. I take it you'll be giving evidence at the trial?'

'No doubt I shall be called,' Waterland answered. 'From the time of Henock's first disappearance, down to the holding of an inquest, I've been a party to this terrible affair. Of course, you may also be called.'

'Indeed so,' the rector agreed. 'But for now I'll leave matters in your very capable hands, Henry, and bid you a good day.'

Chapter Fifteen

For all that Sam Wright enjoyed the occasional excursion as a break from his normal duties in the lawyer's office, he was pleased to see the white stone walls of Walmgate Bar ahead of him on the road. He had changed horses at Bishop Burton, and made progress on the journey, but now dark clouds hanging over the Minster held the promise of imminent rain.

Once through the Bar, he turned left into Piccadilly and stabled his horse at a small inn near the Merchant Adventurers' Hall, where he knew he could get a bite of dinner before setting back to Hedon. Grasping the handles of the Dunns' cloth bag, he threw it over one shoulder and walked along a narrow pathway by the side of the river Fosse, which led directly to the castle precincts. Crossing the Castleyard, he reached the gaol and tugged the bell chain. Tom, the assistant gaoler, opened the door.

''Allo, what you 'ere for?' he asked, inquisitively eyeing up the cloth bag which was now resting at Sam's feet.

Sam did not bother to introduce himself. He had visited the gaol several times in the company of his principal, and the two men knew each other by sight.

'I've a bag of clothes and a letter to deliver to Mistress Alvin,' Sam said.

'Ain't she the lucky one,' Tom sneered sarcastically. 'Friends in 'igh places, 'as she?'

Sam ignored the question. Stepping forward, he deftly pressed a shilling coin into Tom's open hand. The gaoler stepped back and beckoned the clerk inside. Pausing only to close the door, he escorted Sam along the corridors to the cells.

'This is the one,' Tom said, unlocking the two padlocks and, swinging open the cell door, allowed Sam to enter. Mary instantly recognised the lawyer's clerk, as he had frequently assisted Waterland when holding the manor courts at the vicarage.

'Mr Wright,' she exclaimed. 'How good to see you!' Mary looked expectantly behind the clerk, hoping to see more visitors enter, but was taken aback to see Tom close the cell door, leaving them alone. Sam immediately sensed the reason for the obvious disappointment shown on Mary's face.

'I fear the Dunn twins at Patrington are none too well at the moment, so I've been instructed to bring a letter and a few things for you on behalf of the family,' Sam explained.

'Very kind of you, indeed. It's wonderful to see a friendly face in this awful place. But where is my dear sister?'

'I have a letter here from Mistress Anne,' said Sam, ignoring Mary's direct question, and stepped forward to hand the letter over.

Mary began to read the letter, and mid-way through slumped down on the bench. Tears came to her eyes as she read the news of Catherine's death.

'Poor, poor Catherine,' she exclaimed. 'Now I shall never see my dear sister again. Fate has been cruel to us both. She was never in robust health, and here we are in prison, in dire peril, falsely accused.'

'I'm sure all will turn out well,' Sam said sympathetically. 'The assizes begin in about two weeks' time, and I trust that you'll soon be out of this place.'

In truth, Anne's letter had been carefully concocted with the combined skills of draughtsmanship by Henry Waterland and John Pighills. It contained no reference to Adam, nor did it reveal any mention of the discovery of the vicar's body, or the part played in its discovery by Catherine. After describing the circumstances of Catherine's death the remaining paragraphs merely consisted of bland platitudes extolling Mary to be of good heart, and to bear her present indignities with fortitude.

'I believe this parcel contains some items to make life a little more comfortable,' Sam continued, trying his best to raise Mary from her state of low spirits. 'I've also a purse of five pounds, sent by the Dunns and the Pighillses. They all send their love and compliments to you.'

'Are there no plans for them to make a visit?' asked Mary, taking the bag from Sam.

'I fear not,' Sam replied, 'although I know that Mr Waterland will be at York soon and will surely pay a visit.'

Mary examined the contents of the parcel, and was gratified to see a small feather pillow, a bed sheet, a blanket, a bible, and a few items of female apparel.

'I am truly grateful for all the kindness of my friends at Patrington, but I am puzzled there is nothing here to give comfort to my poor husband. Is there no other parcel for Adam?'

Sam shook his head. 'I fear what I have brought here is all that I have been given.'

Mary sighed, and remembered only too well the feelings of animosity which always surrounded her husband when they had all lived in Owthorne.

'So be it,' said Mary at length. 'Please send my heartfelt thanks and love to all my dear friends. Tell them I think of them daily and trust to God that we can come to Patrington soon, free and at peace.'

'Amen to that,' Sam responded, touching his hat, and after giving Mary a polite bow, he called for Tom to release him from the cell.

Left alone with her thoughts, Mary began to consider the situation as it now appeared to be from the news given in Anne's letter. The demise of her sister, for all that she knew, had removed for ever the only witness to the crime. Confident as ever that Catherine would never have broken her solemn vow of silence, and still believing that no trace of her uncle's body had been found, she convinced herself that nothing could be proved against them at the trial. In just two weeks' time, she thought, we shall be free of this nightmare and return to our happy, established way of life back in London.

Sitting alone in the close confines of his cell, bereft of any comforts sent by the Dunns, and unaware of Catherine's death, the thoughts of Adam were very different from those of his wife. All the bitterness and frustrations experienced in his years as a menial servant at Owthorne resurfaced, and he cursed himself for not breaking free when he had had the chance to go to sea. He began to lament of his marriage to Mary, and former feelings of love and passion were slowly replaced by those of sour resentment. In his darkest moments he blamed Mary for the situation in which he now found himself. The days in prison dragged on, and even the occasional arrival of food sent by Daniel Waterland, via Mary's cell, achieved by the usual bribes paid to Tom, did little to lift his utter despair and gloom. Worst of all was the solitude, when hour after hour the same angry thoughts circulated round his tortured mind.

Mary's requests and subsequent pleadings to be allowed to visit her husband were steadfastly refused, or just cruelly ignored by the Chippendales. Even the offer of a substantial bribe was rejected out of hand by Tom, who declared it not worth a candle against the risk of losing his position in the gaol. The pair did have sight of one another on days when services were held in the prison chapel. On these occasions, the few women held in the gaol were shepherded into seats in the centre of the chapel and were allowed the luxury of having their irons removed. Adam and the other male prisoners were then brought into the chapel and seated on outside benches, placed on three sides of the chapel. The men remained in irons throughout, and it was noticeable that extra turnkeys were on duty at chapel times. During these visits Mary took every opportunity she could to steal a glance at Adam; give him a smile of encouragement and blow a silent kiss. Like some naughty child, however, if any of these modest expressions of love were intercepted by Mistress Chippendale, Mary was quickly reprimanded and threatened with an immediate return to her cell.

The chapel services were invariably dull affairs. There was no music or hymn singing allowed, not that any of the prisoners would probably have felt uplifted enough in spirit to sing praises of any kind. Prayers were recited by all in a tone akin to a dirge, and the main part of the service was taken up by a sermon given on some aspect of the inevitable triumph of good over evil. The prison chaplain was the Reverend Mr Charles Mace. Short and round, Mr Mace was grossly overweight. A man in his late sixties, his physical form bore ample witness to a life of over-indulgence. In the field of his clerical vocation, Mr Mace clearly enjoyed the sound of his own voice, and he delivered each homily with great zeal and little regard for the clock.

On the eve of the assizes, Mary was able to bribe Tom to smuggle a note from her to Adam. In the note she was able to relate what circumstances she knew of Catherine's death, and to extol her husband to stand firm at the trial, firmly denying all accusations. Finally, she sent her love and the fervent hope that they would soon resume their old life together in London.

'Good riddance,' was Adam's only thought on learning of Catherine's death. On reflection, he too believed that her passing would give them hope of an acquittal at the trial. However, his former life in London now seemed only a dull memory, and he held no warm aspirations of a return to the capital.

Chapter Sixteen

The assizes at York were a twice-yearly excuse for the Yorkshire nobility and gentry to gather together in the city for a week of gaiety and social intercourse. The High Sheriff of the County acted as master of ceremonies, hosting a number of dinners, glittering balls and other diversions such as horse-racing for the judges and other fashionable visitors.

None of these rich festivities and occasions of pleasure filtered down to the miserable prisoners awaiting trial in their cells at York Castle. There was, however, a heightened sense of anxiety prevailing inside the gaol. This feeling was not calmed in any way by the greedy actions of the Chippendales and Tom to extract as much money as possible from their enforced guests. As the time for the trials approached, it became noticeable that errands and favours were granted more readily. Orders of food were brought in without the usual delays or grumbles, and for a few, friends and relatives were allowed in to see their unfortunate brethren. Exploiting a more unsavoury business, Edmund Chippendale enjoyed a ready source of income by allowing into the gaol a number of local hacks. They appeared regularly at assizes time to talk to the prisoners who were likely to be condemned to death, in order to prepare lurid descriptions of their crimes, which would appear on broadsheets to be sold at a large profit on the morning of their execution. Adam entertained no nonsense of this nature, and shouted violent abuse at the young hack whose pockmarked face appeared pressed to the grill of his cell door. Used to such treatment, the man merely moved to the next cell door, holding up a small silver coin as an inducement to obtain a worthwhile story from the next prisoner.

It was not until the Friday of the week of the assizes that Mary and Adam were finally led from their cells. Fettered only at the wrists, they walked with their chief gaoler and Tom the length of the central corridor, through the communicating rooms and into the entrance hall. There, after the usual exchange of documents, they were handed over to the care of four guards, all dressed in the livery of the High Sheriff. They were then taken out of the gaol and made to walk a short distance to the Moot hall. Then, entering at the rear of the building, they descended a flight of stairs and were escorted into a cheerless room, devoid of all furniture except for benches along three sides.

All efforts made by Mary to talk to Adam were instantly stifled by the guards, who kept the pair apart and imposed a strict silence. At length, after what seemed an agonising delay, the door opened, and they were summoned to climb another flight of stairs. At the top they passed through a narrow doorway and found themselves inside the courtroom. A guard motioned them to move forward towards a stout wooden rail.

'Stand at the bar,' he instructed.

For the first time in weeks, Mary and Adam were together, side by side. For comfort in this new situation, Mary attempted to hold Adam's hand, but he brusquely brushed aside this sign of affection, leaving Mary puzzled and disconcerted. Instead, she was reduced to gazing about her to take in the geography of her new surroundings.

Immediately opposite, raised on a dais, were three figures. The central figure was instantly recognisable as the judge, wearing a gown of vivid scarlet edged with gold. To his left and right sat a man, each dressed in black. Mary correctly surmised that one of the men was a man of the cloth, but she could not identify the third figure, whose black attire was relieved only by a fine white lace neckerchief and cuffs. Immediately below the judge was the judge's clerk, dressed in sombre black, but distinguished from the others by wearing a long black gown, which he gathered about him every time he rose to his feet. To the judge's left, sitting at a small table inside a square-shaped enclosure, was the prosecuting counsel, yet another figure dressed all in black, and, like the clerk, robed with a flowing gown, but in this case with a short wig upon his head, neatly tied at the back with a black ribbon. Completing the principal characters that Mary saw in the courtroom were the jury, sitting in two rows on the judge's right-hand side. In the main, they were dressed in coats, waistcoats, breeches and stockings of a drab brown, grey or plum colour. Mary considered they were ordinary folk, freeholders of the county, chosen from either merchant or farming stock. Permeating the whole atmosphere of the courtroom was an unpleasant smell, reminiscent of rotting vegetables.

Pushing back his chair, the judge's clerk got to his feet and looked at Mary.

'Mary Alvin,' he began, 'you are charged with the crime of wilful murder, contrary to common law, on or about the 10th day of June in the year 1708, of one Henock Sinclare. How say you? Do you plead guilty or not guilty?'

'Not guilty,' replied Mary after a moment's hesitation.

'M'lud,' added the clerk looking straight at Mary.

'I'm sorry - m'lud,' Mary repeated.

The clerk then turned to Adam, and repeating the charge, received the same plea, given in a loud, firm voice.

As if world-weary, the prosecuting counsel slowly got to his feet.

'May it please your Lordship, I appear for the Crown in this case.'

'Very well, we'd better hear it,' said the judge, waving a hand towards counsel and leaning forward to take in the perfume from a nosegay of wild violets set before him.

'Thank you, m'Lord,' returned counsel automatically, and turning to the jury he outlined the case against the prisoners, stating that he wished to bring to the court a number of witnesses, whose testimony would prove beyond any reasonable doubt whatsoever the heinous crime committed by the two prisoners standing at the bar.

Mary and Adam, each in their own separate way, followed the court proceedings intently. On hearing counsel mention the word 'witnesses', Mary was nonplussed as to who could possibly give evidence against them. Her naïveté was soon cruelly exposed as worthless as, one by one, familiar figures from the past came into court and gave their evidence. It remained only for counsel to weave together all this evidence to manufacture a damning case against the pair.

First on the stand was young George Dunn. Under oath he related to the judge and jury how he had placed Catherine in front of him on his horse and how she had dropped her glove on the spot where the vicar's body was subsequently found. Mary was aghast at this revelation, and looked at Adam. He did not meet Mary's eyes and stared resolutely ahead, the colour draining from his face. Out of the side of his mouth, in a low whisper, he snarled, 'I hope she burns in hell!'

The discovery and identification of the body of Henock Sinclare was confirmed by John Jordan and Samuel Owbridge, each in turn taking the stand in the witness box. The court was then regaled with a gruesome description of the state of the victim's skull by the apothecary, Leonard Tymm.

Up to this point the judge had not intervened in the proceedings, remaining silent, but on hearing Tymm's graphic description he interrupted counsel with a question to the witness.

'No doubt, therefore, that a wilful murder has taken place?'

'None at all, my Lord.'

'Would you tell the court how death might have been caused.'

'I should say by a blow from some sharp instrument, my Lord, perhaps an axe or a hedge slasher.'

'Extreme force used in making the blow, would you say?'

'Yes, my Lord.'

'Capable of being administered by a woman?'

'Rather unlikely, my Lord,' concluded Tymm, who was then allowed to leave the stand.

To the amazement of the two accused, the next witness called was Sarah Handson. Four years had passed since they had last seen her, and in the meantime she had blossomed into a fully-formed young woman in her mid-teens. Her contribution to the prosecution's case was to relate how she had been given an errand to return home on the eve of the disappearance of the vicar. She explained that this kept her away from the vicarage until the next day, a matter which counsel correctly suggested to the jury was a ruse to remove an unwanted witness to a crime about to take place. On the stand, Sarah looked across with pity at her former mistress, and gave her testimony in a faltering voice. Choked with emotion, she was dismissed by counsel and left the courtroom in tears.

Next on the stand was Grimston Cookman. He obviously enjoyed his moment in the limelight, and gave animated accounts of finding the vicar's horse, the fruitless searches for the missing man, and the subsequent discovery of Henock Sinclare's whip and wig on the cliff top at Holmpton. Cookman was then asked to stand down, and was replaced by the familiar figure of the Reverend John Pighills. He was able to confirm all the previous evidence given of digging up the body of his old friend, but touched new ground when he described how Mary had wished to marry Adam, against the wishes of her uncle. He testified to the moody and sullen nature of the servant, and painted a black picture of a man of low station, eager for advancement by marriage but frustrated in his desire by the obstinacy of his master.

This damning description was confirmed by no less a person than Henry Waterland, who proved to be the last witness called by the prosecuting counsel. He recounted to the court the details of his interview with Adam soon after the disappearance of the vicar, emphasising the arrogance of the servant and his seemingly callous behaviour in the absence of his master. Waterland was able to tell the jury of the secret marriage which Mary and Adam had undertaken at Halsham, barely three months after the disappearance of the vicar. Finally, he told of their 'escape' from Holderness and the circumstances of their arrest at the Black Swan in Holborn.

At the judge's bidding, counsel began to sum up the case against the accused. The barrister confidently put forward to the jury a reconstruction of what he believed had taken place in and around the Owthorne vicarage that June day four years previously. With only minor deviations from the truth, the pair listened with mounting fear and dread. Equally distressful to Mary, standing beside her husband, was the realisation that all his former feelings of love for her had evaporated after hearing of Catherine's fatal indiscretion in the vicarage yard.

The judge's summing up was short, but to the independent observer, fair and balanced. He emphasised to the jury that there were no living witnesses to the crime, pointing out the unfortunate decease of the accused's sister, who must have known what had taken place, as she had revealed to witnesses the place of burial of the murdered man. Much of the evidence heard, he remarked, had been of a circumstantial nature, and he warned the jury against accepting counsel's plausible suggestions as to what 'might have happened' regarding the stated testimony of objections to the marriage by the murdered vicar. He then sent the jury away to consider their verdict and adjourned the court.

Mary and Adam were led down the steps and taken back to the room below stairs. Mercifully, some bread and water was provided. Adam sullenly kept his gaze on the floor, and gave no sign of recognition to Mary as he slowly ate his portion of bread and drank from a pewter mug. Mary looked at her husband in a state of desperation. She felt abandoned, and was full of anguish as to what would happen next.

'Won't be long now,' said one of the guards, almost cheerfully. 'With so many cases to get through today this judge don't allow 'em much time to ponder.'

True to the guard's prediction, little more than half an hour passed by before they were called up to the courtroom. The judge's clerk rose to address the foreman of the jury and requested him to stand up.

'In the case of Mary Alvin, here accused, are you agreed on your verdict? Do you find the prisoner guilty or not guilty?'

'Not guilty, sir.'

'Is that the verdict of you all?'

'It is, sir.'

An enormous wave of emotion flooded over Mary, and she almost fainted with relief, only steadying herself from falling by grasping the rail of the bar in front of her. She forced herself to look at Adam, but his eyes were riveted on the clerk as he again addressed the foreman.

'In the case of Adam Alvin, here accused, are you agreed on your verdict? Do you find the prisoner guilty or not guilty?'

'Guilty, sir.'

'And is that the verdict of you all?'

The words of the foreman's affirmation were drowned by Adam, who began to shout out at the top of his voice and waved his fettered hands above his head in supplication to the judge.

'I'm innocent,' he screamed. 'I never did 'im no 'arm. No 'arm at all. They've lied to you, all these people.' He looked around wildly and fixed his eyes on the prosecuting barrister.

It took some time before order was restored in the courtroom. For this to happen it required two of the guards, one on each side, to restrain Adam from crossing the bar.

In all the upheaval of this wild outburst Mary found herself pushed to one side, but when all was relatively calm again, she realised that the judge was looking directly at her.

'Mary Alvin, you have been acquitted by the jury of the charge. You are therefore discharged and may go free.'

One of the guards took Mary's arm and led her back down the now familiar steps. As she left the courtroom her last sight of Adam was of a desperate figure struggling to break free from the grasp of the remaining guards.

'Adam Alvin,' continued the judge in a solemn voice, ignoring the commotion still prevailing. 'You have been found guilty of the crime of wilful murder. Have you anything to say before sentence is passed on you?'

'I'm not guilty,' shouted Adam, 'not guilty your Lordship.'

'Yes, yes,' said the judge testily. 'We've heard all this already.'

The judge reached to one side and placed a small square of black cloth upon his head.

'The sentence of this court is that you be taken from here to a convenient place of execution and hanged by the neck until you are dead. So help you God.'

'Amen,' said the cleric sitting at the judge's side.

'Take him down,' commanded the judge, and all watched as the guards, with difficulty, propelled Adam away from the bar, down the steps and back to the gaol.

* * * * *

Mary walked back to the entrance hall of the gaol in the company of her guards. Still in a state of shock and bewilderment at the events which had just taken place in the courtroom, she barely acknowledged the presence of Edmund Chippendale and Tom waiting in the hall.

'All gone well for you then,' sneered the chief gaoler sarcastically. 'You'll be wanting to be free of these, no doubt,' he said, holding up the irons securing Mary's hands. As Mary waited for Chippendale to unlock the fetters, Mistress Chippendale appeared, carrying Mary's clothes and bedding from the cell, all wrapped up in a sheet. She placed them at Mary's feet without a word spoken.

'That'll be six and eight pence for us, Ma'am, and two shillings for Tom here,' Chippendale said.

Mary, now released from her chains and with a sudden surge of rage, turned on her former gaoler.

'I'm proved innocent,' she cried. 'You've no right to take any more money from me. You've had enough already!'

''Fraid not,' replied Chippendale impassively. 'It's the law, them's standard discharge fees and there'll be no leaving this place till we receive payment.

Chippendale stood his ground with a look on his face that told Mary he meant every word uttered. Mary snorted with anger, but she needed only one second to consider the situation. In truth, she would happily pay twice the amount demanded to be free from that detested place; to breathe fresh air again, to be without fetters and to walk the streets freely. The gaoler's demands were naught but a pittance against the wages of her liberty. She searched in her purse and slapped the coins into Chippendale's open palm. Picking up the bundle of clothes, she turned abruptly and walked through the open doors into the courtyard. For all that the act of walking after weeks of confinement was painful, she maintained a brave step and made straight for the castle gateway, gaining physical strength and mental confidence with every step taken.

'But what am I to do?' she said to herself as she walked away from the gaol. She had lost her husband for ever. She had little money left, and certainly no friends she could turn to for aid in Holderness. After a few moments of self-pity, her old determination returned, and with a gesture of defiance she tossed the bundle of clothes into the murky waters of the river Fosse.

'I know what I'll do,' she said to herself. 'I'll go to the Black Swan here in Coney Street. I may not have enough money for the journey, but I know all the coachmen on the run. They'll see me safely back to London.'

With raised spirits and an invigorated step, she headed towards Castlegate, in the direction of Coney Street.

Chapter Seventeen

In the gaol, battered and bruised from his altercation with the guards, Adam slumped down on the bench in one of the condemned cells. Edmund Chippendale stood over him whilst Tom clamped heavy irons round his ankles.

'Not long to wait,' said Chippendale, adopting the role of mock comforter. 'It'll be the drop at the "Three-legged Mare" on Monday. 'Course, we can make these last days a tidy bit more comfortable for you – a little coal and wood, perhaps?' He waved a hand in the direction of an empty, cheerless stove situated in the corner of the cell. 'For a mite extra, we can fetch a tasty meal or two. We don't want you looking starved when you go out, do we?'

'Burn in 'ell,' Adam retorted sullenly.

'I'll wager you'll be first of us there,' said the gaoler with a smirk upon his face. 'Please yourself. It's a barley loaf a day and water, then, is it? Pity, really, a small gratuity could make things a deal more comfortable.'

Chippendale again pointed to the stove, but not receiving any response from Adam, he shrugged his shoulders, and the two gaolers left the condemned man alone in the cell.

Bitterness engulfed Adam as he contemplated his ill fortune over and over again in his head. He placed all the blame for his plight on both the Sinclare sisters. In the years of his youth, living at the vicarage, he had never been close to Catherine. She had always been reserved in her dealings with him, and never once had she shown him any real signs of affection. In the past he assigned much of this lack of feeling down to her bad health, and with the compensation of love given by Mary, he had previously suffered no great feelings of deprivation by Catherine's detached and reserved behaviour. Now he felt betrayed by her devious action in revealing the whereabouts of the body of Henock Sinclare. The careful way in which Catherine had managed to keep her vow of silence unbroken by the unspoken deed, carried out with George Dunn on horseback, was of no consolation or moral value to the doomed man. She had betrayed him, and she was the main cause of his ruin.

The blame which he attached to Mary was centred on the cunning of her female guile in holding him back, forcing him to remain at the vicarage. He had been her prisoner in a futile pact of love, when he wanted to be free, enjoying a life at sea, with all the adventures that that would have entailed. Such miserable thoughts were virtually all the company Adam entertained throughout the evenings of his last Friday and Saturday. The only interruption to his solitary meditations was the appearance, once a day, of Tom bringing a loaf of bread and a pitcher of water. The bread was hard to swallow, and the water tasted brackish, but Adam was resolute in a stubborn defiance not to pass over his last few coins to his greedy gaoler.

Sunday morning brought both Chippendale and Tom early to the condemned cell. Tom checked Adam's irons, after which they escorted him, slowly dragging his chains along the stone corridor, to the chapel for the customary Lord's Day service. Sitting along the wall, Adam noted two other fellows, similarly shackled, and clearly in the same condemned situation as himself. He also noticed an increased number of the sheriff's guards on duty, two of whom he recognised as being present at the trial. Idly, he wondered if any man had ever managed to escape from this prison.

The Reverend Mr Charles Mace opened the service with the usual recital of prayers. He intoned the words quite automatically, without feeling, and with his eyes raised up to an earthly ceiling. A few readings from the Scriptures followed, all apparently selected for their message extolling the moral value of good over evil. The readings over, Mr Mace launched into his sermon. The rotund cleric took his opening text from Genesis: 'Whoso sheddeth man's blood, by man shall his blood be shed.' This was soon reinforced by reference to the fifth commandment, and then, working himself up to a high state of oratory, he moved on to Revelations:

'And the sea gave up the dead which were in it, and death and hell delivered up the dead which were in them; and they were judged every man according to their works.'

At this point, Adam, who hitherto had paid little attention to the service, realised sharply that the speaker was addressing the sermon directly at him, and when the man reached the point of giving graphic details of evildoers, as souls without hope, doomed to everlasting despair in the fires of hell, Adam could sit silent no longer. Rising to his feet and shaking his manacled hands at the cleric, he cried out with all his might.

'I'm innocent, you old fool!' he cried. 'I'm innocent, do you 'ear? Let me loose, I'm innocent!'

Momentarily, all eyes turned round to see who had made this unscheduled interruption. Then the noise of a low groan was heard from the pulpit, causing the attention of all present to move from Adam and back to Mr Mace. The colour of the cleric's round face had flushed to a deep red, his hands clutched his chest, and in virtual slow-motion, he collapsed to the ground, falling out of sight, down to the floor of the pulpit. For a second or two, nobody moved, but all stared at the seemingly empty pulpit in frank amazement. It was only a short moment of calm, however, as Chippendale and two guards rushed up to the pulpit. With considerable difficulty, they were able to pull the corpulent figure of the cleric out from the confines of the pulpit. By this time the redness of his face had faded, and the appearance of his periwig, knocked askew, and now only covering one half of his bald head, gave a strange, almost comical aspect to the fallen figure. It was clear to all in the chapel, however, that this was no act or scene of comedy. The reverend exhibited no signs of life. A kneeling Edmund Chippendale was heard to say, 'God help him – he's gone!'

Gasps of astonishment reverberated around the chapel. Adam quickly overcame his own sense of surprise and seized this unexpected opportunity with relish.

'You see,' he shouted at the top of his voice. 'A sign from God. I'm innocent. Let me go free, or they'll all be struck down by the hand of God, like this fellow 'ere!'

One or two audible 'Amens' came from around the room, and then as the volume of excited voices began to increase, a number of the women prisoners rose to their feet, convinced they had witnessed a clear sign from God, shouting, 'Glory be, he's innocent,' and 'Free the man!' Even those of a more sceptical nature, and unconvinced of having witnessed a revelation from the Almighty, quickly joined in the demonstration, enjoying a diversion from the usual drudgery of prison life, and greatly adding to the din and confusion.

'Get 'em all out of here. Get 'em back to the cells!' Chippendale shouted to Tom, and although he was still holding up the lifeless form of Mr Mace, he was able to wave with his one free arm to call the guards to assist with the removal of the prisoners. Two guards seized Adam and roughly forced him back to the condemned cell.

It was almost eight o'clock on the Monday morning when the bolts on Adam's cell door were drawn back and the door opened. A young man, dressed in the familiar garb of a cleric, stood at the threshold. He introduced himself as the Reverend Mr Jeremy Brown, a curate from the Church of the Holy Trinity in Micklegate. He explained to Adam that it was his duty to accompany the condemned to the scaffold that morning, in place of Mr Mace. Adam half-listened to the curate's explanation, and gruffly refused his offer of saying a prayer together.

'Get on with your business,' he said darkly, on seeing Chippendale standing in the doorway behind the curate.

'One moment, please,' interrupted the curate. 'I have known in the past, that on these sad occasions it helps to ease one's conscience to leave this sinful world having made a clean breast of all that has gone on before. Would you like to clear your conscience of all such matters before we go?'

Adam shrugged his shoulders in a final sign of capitulation. He saw that nothing now would save him from his fate, and all further pretence of innocence was useless.

'If it pleases you,' he said, with a sigh. 'Yes, I killed that selfish old man and well 'e deserved it. Now let's 'ave an end to all your questions.'

For the last time Adam was led down the corridor, through the connecting rooms, the entrance hall and out into the castle yard. Looking ahead, he was quite unprepared for the sight which met his eyes. Immediately in front of the gaol was a horse-drawn cart carrying long boxes. Already sitting on two of the boxes were the men he had seen on the previous day in the chapel. In front and behind the cart were rows of the sheriff's men in full uniform, each holding a halberd mounted on a long pole. At the head of the procession were two mounted officers carrying drawn swords over their shoulders. Hampered by his leg irons, Adam was lifted into the cart by two of the Sheriff's men. As he sat down on the third, vacant box, he realised from the odd shape that it was a coffin. Tom climbed up on the cart and removed Adam's wrist irons. Swiftly, he moved to pinion the arms tightly behind the prisoner's back. At a command from one of the officers, the procession moved off and headed for the open castle gate.

Leaving the castle precincts, the procession was met by a crowd of noisy citizens, some of whom began to blow horns or beat improvised tin drums, creating an unearthly din. A groundswell of morbid hilarity quickly took hold of the crowd as they marched along behind the official party. Sellers of broadsheets mingled with the crowd, finding ready purchasers eager to read the concocted stories of the lives and crimes of the two other men sitting in the cart.

Vendors, carrying trays of ha'penny sugar buns and warm, penny meat pies, were also doing a lively trade, as the mob accompanied the condemned through Micklegate Bar and on the road towards the Knavesmire.

Adam looked away from the scene, feeling nothing but disgust and contempt for those following. He looked briefly at his two involuntary companions on the cart, but felt no pity for them. All his remaining store of compassion he reserved for himself, and did his best to ignore the ribald shouts from the mob by staring blankly ahead. Faced with the inevitable, he was determined to show some outward signs of courage at the end. Even so, a feeling of dread entered all the sinews of his body as the cart came to a standstill under the "Three-legged Mare" of the York Tyburn.

'Stand if you will, gentlemen,' ordered one of the officers, but none in the cart obeyed the command. Instantly, several guards climbed on the cart, forcing the prisoners to their feet. In quick succession, halters were placed around their necks and the ropes thrown over the horizontal beams of the triangular-shaped instrument of execution.

Adam did not listen to the officer reading out the sentences, nor did he hear the prayers recited by the curate. He was aware, however, of an officer giving a final order. An expectant hush fell upon the crowd, and Adam felt the cart jolt forward. He closed his eyes and fixed his thoughts on that voyage at sea. The movement became the rise and fall of the Billy Boy against the waves, with the cries of the gulls circling above and a strong sea breeze pulling him sideways. He felt free at last . . .

Epilogue: Murder by the Sea – Separating Fact from Fiction

The story told in *Murder by the Sea* is largely based on historical fact. Henock Sinclare was the vicar of Owthorne from 1681 until his tragic death in 1708. He did live at the Owthorne vicarage with his two Sinclare nieces and a manservant called Adam Alvin. He was murdered on 10 June 1708 and an inquest on his death, held almost four years later, brought in a verdict of unlawful murder by Adam Alvin. We know that Alvin and the elder niece, Mary Sinclare, married by licence at Halsham less than three months after the crime, and additionally there is strong hearsay evidence to testify that Alvin went to the gallows at York for his crime. So what represents fact and what represents fiction in the story?

Firstly, we know that the Sinclare family came from Kilham, a sizeable market town on the East Yorkshire Wolds, four miles to the north-east of Driffield. When Henock Sinclare was born at Kilham on 10 March 1657, the son of David Sinclare and his second wife, Lucy, he came from a family of well-established freehold farmers. Although born of farming stock, one of his uncles, also called Henock, became a cleric and was appointed vicar of New Malton in North Yorkshire. When the uncle died in 1678, not only did he leave the usual grants of money to the poor – in this case, at both New Malton and Kilham, but he also made a number of bequests to nephews and nieces. Amongst these was the gift of his books and ten shillings to the young Henock.

According to the volume *Alumni Cantabrigiensis*, the young Henock went to Kilham school, but at the age of fourteen, on 26 January 1672, he was admitted a sizar at St John's College. He graduated with a bachelor's degree in 1676 and became a Master of Arts in 1679. Ordained a priest at York in December 1680, he was inducted as vicar of Owthorne on 17 April 1681. This proved to be his only clerical appointment, and he stayed at Owthorne until his untimely death in 1708.

Some of the detail of the Sinclare family may be deduced from the will of Henock's mother, Lucy, written on 1 January 1671. From this document we learn that Lucy was a widow of some standing at Kilham. Her eldest son George received a bequest of four oxgangs of land in the Northside fields there, and her daughter was to receive the substantial sum of thirty pounds. The residue of the estate was divided between her three sons, George, 'Enock' (seen on this document without the 'H') and Samuel, who were all appointed joint executors of the will. More family linkages may be deduced from entries in the Kilham parish registers, although the repetition of the Christian names of George and David makes absolute identity in some cases difficult to establish.

Henock Sinclare's presentation to the church of Owthorne is splendidly recorded in a memorandum written by himself in the parish register book. The ceremony was completed by his reading of the thirty-nine articles and by declaring his assent 'to everything contained in the Book of Common Prayer'. The memorandum was signed by Henock, his two churchwardens, John Jegger and George Gibson, and witnessed by five other parishioners, all five of whom were only able to make their mark. Other relevant documentation written during the lifetime of Henock Sinclare is hard to find. Of course, the usual periodic entries of baptisms, burials and marriages appear in the Owthorne parish registers; however, these vital events were not frequent. The last recorded entry by Henock was the baptism of Mary, the daughter of James Atkinson dated 11 December 1707.

One early notice of the man occurred in October 1680, when his signature appears as one of the witnesses on the conveyance indenture of a number of closes in Hedon; the vendor being Alderman Richard Barne and the purchaser Alderman William Baines, the future father-in-law of the Hedon lawyer, Henry Waterland.

Far more relevant to the telling of this story is, 'A Terrier of all such Glebe and other rights as doe belong to the Vicaridge [sic] of Owthorne', written for an Archbishop's visitation by Henock and his two churchwardens, Matthew Preston and Robert Haggitt, in October 1685. This document gives a good description of the vicarage house, the stables and gardens, and explains the endowments relating to the benefice. In total, the living was valued, 'sometimes more, sometimes less', at £50 per year, a fairly modest sum for a South Holderness parish.

A little later, and perhaps reflecting Henock's clerical status in the deanery of Holderness, is recorded in the Winestead parish register:

In 1689 George Longmire, Parson, was inducted by Mr. Henock Sinclare, Vic. of Owthorne.

Of particular interest is a document found in the archive of the East Riding's Quarter Sessions. This is dated 10 September 1707 and relates to Henock being bound over to keep the peace and to appear at the next Quarter Sessions to answer charges brought against him by his servant William Hutton. The outcome of Henock's appearance at Beverley is not known, and I could find no trace of a Hutton in the Owthorne parish registers. Some glimpse of Hutton's character, however, may be gleaned from a postscript written by the JP, William Lister, on the Recognizance:

These may Certify that the same Day and year aboves'd, the sd. Willm Hutton was Convicted before me for swearing one Profane Oath.
Witness my Hand.
Wm Lister.

In chronological order, the next documentary source of significance is the marriage entry of Adam Alvin and Mary Sinclare in the parish register of All Saints Church at Halsham. According to the work of 1911, *A History of Withernsea* by G T J Miles and W Richardson, the entry reads:

Adam Alvin and Mary Sinclare, both of the Parish of Owthorne, were maryd. In the Parish Church of Halsham pr. License August the 29th. 1708.

When the author examined this register in 2006, he found that more than one half of the entry had been blotted out by an ink spill. It was, however, clearly not an act of discrimination against known criminals, but the result of an accident, or at worst, deliberate vandalism on a general nature, as several entries in the register showed similar obliterations.

Post the murder survive a number of documents which shine some light on the unfolding story. Very frustratingly a few are undated, but it is clear that David Sinclare of Kilham obtained letters of administration at York for the 'Goods, Rights, Creditts, Cattells and Chattells' of his deceased half-brother. In an undated account drawn up by David it would appear that some silver items, a tankard, spoon and wine taster were stolen from the empty vicarage. In the event the thief was caught and conveyed forty miles to York Castle gaol. David also paid £2 to several persons who were employed:

. . . to search and look in the Ditches and Pownds at Severall times for the body of the deceased which as yet has not been found or heard of.

This last statement would indicate that the account was written some time after the murder (10 June 1708) and before the discovery of the body (18 April 1712).

No doubt contemporary with the above is a memorandum, dated 27 April 1710, entered into the Owthorne parish register. At the request of David Sinclare, two clergymen, supported by no fewer than eight witnesses, one of whom being John Jordan, the churchwarden, came to Owthorne and testified that the vicarage house was 'found very insuffic[ien]t', and that one of the beast houses 'was utterly Demolished'.

A final source of information in this immediate post-murder period is the vicar's post mortem inventory, a document which is neither dated nor records the names of the four appraisers. His goods were valued at the relatively low figure of £121 3s. 0d, but outstanding debts, together with those already collected by David Sinclare, added a further £167 17s. 10d. The list of debtors' names clearly shows that the vicar was in the habit of giving financial help to many in the district. One of the outstanding loans, worth £10, was against an 'Elizabeth Piggells', who may well have been the real wife of the rector of Patrington Church.

Almost four years after the marriage of Alvin and Mary, the parish register of Owthorne then takes up the story with the first evidence of the murder. A burial entry by the new vicar, the Reverend Richard Sissison, dated 23 April 1712, states:

Mr. Henock Sinclare Vicar of Owthorn Buried in the South-Isle that joins on the Chancel. He was murdered by his Man=Servt. Adam Alvin June 10th. 1708 and laid concealed in the Ground in a Pit abt. five Yards from the Vicarage House till the 18th. April 1712 - & upon the 20th. of the same Month was found upon the Inquest of the Coroner & Jury to be so murdered by the Person aforesaid.

After 1712 oral history played its part in keeping alive the story of the murder for over seventy years. However, in 1735 a related reference appeared in Thomas Gent's published book, *The History of the Royal and Beautiful Town of Kingston-upon-Hull*. In the book Gent described the appointment in 1715 of a Rev Mr Charles Mace to the position of vicar of Holy Trinity Church at Hull. Gent went on to say:

This Gentleman's Father dy'd in the Pulpit: For as he was preaching in York Castle to the condemn'd Prisoners (who were to be executed the Day following) one of them was so harden'd, as openly to interrupt, and even defy him, in that Part of the Discourse, that hinted at his Crime: Which unparalell'd Audacity so deeply pierc'd the tender Minister to the heart, whose melting Oratory was pathetically employ'd in moving the unhappy Wretches to repent of their crying Sins, whereby to obtain Divine Mercy that he instantly fainted away, dropt down and departed this Life . . .

From later sources we know that this 'harden'd prisoner' was in fact Adam Alvin, and Gent gave further proof in a footnote:

The Criminal had barbarously murdered a Clergyman, who was his Wife's uncle and bury'd him in a Field, where he was found by the berateing of his own Dog: Yet the Wretch received the Sacrament as a Token of his innocency; said that Mr. Mace's death was a judgement upon him for supposing him guilty; and did not confess until the Moment he was going to be turned off the Ladder.

Gent's claim that the body of the vicar was discovered by his own dog finds no support in any other version of the story, but in all other respects his facts dovetail with those from later sources. Gent put the death of the Rev Mr Charles Mace senior down 'to about the Year 1711', but we know it must have been slightly later, as Henock Sinclare's body was not discovered until April 1712.

Concerning the capture and incarceration of Adam and Mary in York Castle gaol, no documentary evidence has been found by this author. Similarly a blank was drawn over the trial proceedings at York Assizes, in spite of a careful search in the National Archives at Kew. Sadly, the volume ASSI 44 (indictments) has a note stating, '. . . the records were complete except for large gaps between 1700 and 1721'. Equally frustrating is the fact that the *York Courant* newspaper, which could have reported on local executions, was not in circulation until 1725. Only one document has been found which gives conclusive proof of the trial of the couple at York. This again is sourced from the East Riding Quarter Sessions archive held at Beverley. Addressed to the Riding's JPs, it concerns the petition of Samuel Owbridge of Owthorne, who was ordered by the magistrate, William Lister, to appear at York Assizes, 'to give evidence against Adam Alvin and Mary his Wife for the Murder of Henock Sinclare, Clerk'. The petitioner pleaded to say that he did give evidence at the trial and stayed there four days for the purpose. In addition, Lister ordered that Owbridge should transport Lucy Sinclare, spinster, another witness at the trial, back from York to Hull and pay for her expenses on the journey.

Understandably, Owbridge's petition to the justices was to seek compensation for all his travelling expenses, which included the hire of a horse. The JPs duly obliged and ordered that Owbridge was to receive one pound from the public purse, '. . . as charity in respect of his poverty'. Unbelievably, the document is not dated.

Sometime about 1785 the Reverend William Dade collected the essentials of the tale from an unknown source and wrote them down under the simple heading of 'A Murder'. Dade was born at Burton Agnes in 1740, the son of the Reverend Thomas Dade, rector of that parish. Ordained at York in 1763, three years later he was presented to the rectory of Barmston in the north of Holderness. Being an antiquarian of some distinction, he announced his intention to write a history of Holderness, and set about the task of collecting information for the project. Unfortunately, ill-health prevented the completion of this work and he died at Barmston on 2 August 1790. Fortunately, Dade's manuscripts were purchased by William Constable and placed by him in his library at Burton Constable.

The story of the murder as written by William Dade reveals several new facts about the case. Dade confirmed the presence of five people living in the vicarage house; the vicar, the two nieces and two domestics, a male and female. Adam Alvin is described as a manservant, 'now about 25 years of age'. He is given the blame for devising the plot to kill the vicar and for communicating 'the black design to the two sisters, who scrupled not to be accomplices in his guilt'. The ruse of Adam leaving the vicar's horse saddled and bridled in the neighbourhood is related here, as are the growing suspicions of foul play by the locals. Dade has the date of the couple marrying at Halsham in the margin of the paper, and speaks of

The newly married Pair, alarmed for their safety, attempted by leaving the Country, to fly from Justice & sought to dissipate the terrors of their guilty minds in a crowded Metropolis.

Dade described the part played by the younger sister in the discovery of the body of her uncle, only by saying:

Arrested by a sudden & fatal sickness, exhibited dreadful perturbations of Mind and unable to articulate, she intimated by forcible & expressive signs, where the Body of her Uncle might be found.

It is frustrating that there are no real details recorded of how the guilty pair were arrested in London. The narrative simply states:

Such was the Spirit & activity of the neighbourhood that in a short time they penetrated into the secret recesses of the Metropolis, in order to be arraigned.

The remainder of Dade's written account covers the given verdicts at the trial; the death of the Reverend Mr Mace during the service at York Castle gaol on the day before the execution; Adam's final confession and his execution. Of course, we now wish that Dade had recorded more details of the story. Important, large gaps are apparent; for example, nowhere does he give a name to the younger sister. There is no mention either of the discovery of any whip, wig or hat left by Alvin on the cliff top, or the part played by David Sinclare after the murder of his half-brother. We learn nothing of the whereabouts of the younger sister after Mary and Adam had fled to London. However, we must be grateful for what William Dade did record and pass on to the next source. But before doing so, it is relevant to add a postscript of general historical interest concerning Dade's manuscripts. These lay untouched in the Burton Constable library for over fifty years. About the year 1838, Sir T A Clifford Constable allowed George Poulson, the author of *Beverlac*, a history of Beverley, to have use of them in order to complete the history which William Dade had proposed back in 1783. Poulson virtually repeated Dade's narrative of the murder, limiting himself to minor editorial changes. He added no new facts to the story written down by Dade.

Some thirteen years before Poulson published his *History and Antiquities of the Seigniory of Holderness* in 1840, a Withernsea resident wrote a fascinating account of the story for James Iveson, the Town Clerk of Hedon. His narrative adds a number of details and reads as follows: (Original spellings used throughout. Author's collection)

Mr. Enoch Sinclare was Vicar of Owthorn 30 years. John Westerdale & Richd Fenby knew the woman who so [sic] him Taken up out of the place where he was Concealed and she said that she never Could Eate any Brains of any kind after; her name was Ann Gargill. She died in the 100 Year of her Age; the report was he was Murdered with Spade and his Skull was laid Open: and the man Adam Alvin took his Horse and Hat & Whip as far as Whitin Holm near a well to prevent any Suspision; his Coffin Sliped down Cliff from the South Isle of the Church about 12 years ago; and it was reinterred in the Low part of Church Yard being a lead one and is near Cliff again.
There was two Nieces lived with him at the time he was Murdered and Adam Alvin wanted to Marrey one of them and they Got Maried after and went to Lincolnshire and kept a publick House at the time he was taken the report was the Other nice [sic] Could not rest well untill She made a discovery by droping a glove on the place where

he was Concealed. The man was tried by a Coronor inquest and Hanged.

Withernsea July 1. 1827

I remain Your Most Obt.

Richd Fenby

Under Fenby's signature, written in pencil by an unknown hand, probably much later than 1827, was added:

Here are nothing about the oath not to tell and how she rode behind a man who was to ride through the yard and as they crossed the place she dropped her glove but did not tell etc. etc.

This is the first detailed mention of the younger sister's role in revealing the location of the vicar's body. However, her action is explained more clearly in another note found together with Fenby's memorandum amongst James Iveson's papers. The note is in the Hedon lawyer's own handwriting and states:

The tradition is that the other niece knowing of the Murder swore or vowed to her sister never to tell of it. Her conscience, however, sore troubled her & on some occasion, she, by word or deed created suspicion and being much pressed to reveal what she knew, she contrived it to be understood that she would give some token and when behind some one on horseback crossing the place where the body had been concealed, she significantly dropped her glove on the spot.

No date appears on this note but as Iveson added the instruction, 'may this be added to the annexed', ie Fenby's memorandum, then it would appear to be of similar date.

Two accounts of the murder, written after the time that Poulson wrote his *History of Holderness*, are worth mentioning. The first was a magazine article by the well-known East Riding author and artist, T Tindall Wildridge. His account entitled 'A Tale of Crime' appeared in the *Hull Illustrated Journal* in 1888.

Wildridge's article occupies eight pages of the Journal and tells the story in rather melodramatic terms, a style which suited the Victorian readers of the day. Strangely, he names the two nieces as Catherine and Anne, with the former being the one to marry Adam. Some of the facts given are clearly inventions of the author; for example, Wildridge has Adam forcing both nieces to swear oaths, 'never to divulge what you have heard or seen this day', following the murder. He also has Adam turning out the vicar's 'old white horse' on the road to Paull, which seems quite baffling, as Paull is at least ten miles from Owthorne. He does, however, have the vicar's hat and wig, 'thrown in such a situation as to induce a belief that he (the vicar) had fallen from the cliff into the sea'.

Quite fancifully, Wildridge has his 'Catherine' falling ill in London and wanting to see her younger sister 'Anne', 'the load of her husband's guilt lying heavy upon her'. He then has Adam travelling north by coach and boat to Patrington Haven, to implore Anne to go back with him to London to see her sister. This request is refused and leads Anne, under pressure from her Patrington friends, to reveal the whereabouts of the vicar's body.

Finally, Wildridge has 'Catherine' present at Adam's execution. Quite out of character, when at the gallows, he sees his wife and kisses her, 'with tears streaming in torrents from his eyes . . .'

In spite of Wildridge's very colourful and highly inaccurate account, I'm grateful to him for introducing for the first time the story of the shipwreck at Owthorne and Henock Sinclare's rescue of the tiny baby from the lifeless form of his mother. This, I believe, greatly adds to the drama of the story.

The second account of note is much more factual and appears as an appendix in G T J Miles and William Richardson's *A History of Withernsea*, published in 1911.

Miles and Richardson correctly call the elder niece Mary, and give the name of Catherine to the younger girl, a style which I have adopted in the story. The two authors repeat the tale of Adam's arrival from the shipwreck, quoting the source as 'local tradition'. They also repeat all the salient points of the story, saying that they have relied 'upon the entries in the Parish Registers and tradition which has handed down various versions of the affair'.

The authors do, however, add one interesting piece of new evidence culled from the Owthorne Overseers' Book. This book records that on 4 May 1708 Henock Sinclare was in possession of property with an annual rateable value of £12. They go on to state:

In the year after the murder, Mr Sinclair's [sic] name drops out and the name Adam Alvin appears but ceases in 1711. From this it would seem that Alvin, in the right of his wife, came into some little property on the death of the vicar.

So ends the story of the murder of the vicar of Owthorne, and one suspects that unless some hitherto unknown document comes to light, that is all we shall ever know of the true events. Nevertheless, one cannot help but speculate if Mary and Adam produced any children during their four years of marriage together. No subsequent report has ever suggested the birth of any child from the union, nor has there been any revelation of where Mary may have gone after her acquittal at the York assizes.

If we assume that the story of Adam's arrival at Owthorne in a shipwreck was an invention of Wildridge's creative imagination, both his true coming and his origins are unknown. Dr David Neave kindly pointed out to me that a certain Adam Alvin married a Rebecca Thompson at Goxhill in North Lincolnshire on 16 October 1661. It is hypothetically possible that this man could have been Adam's father, but this is, of course, pure speculation.

The surname 'Alvin' does occur in several Holderness parish registers during the eighteenth century. Between the years 1754 and 1761 the Owthorne parish register has entries concerning a John and William Alvin, conceivably brothers, and the baptisms of their daughters. It is difficult to believe, however, that any direct descendants of the murderer of 1708 would live in the same village only forty-six years after the event.

Also found are Jonathan Alvin of Ottringham, who has a will in probate in May 1744, and Henry Alvin of Holmpton, who appears in a York probate entry for September 1738. It is likely that it was Henry's daughter Susannah who was married at St Augustine's church at Hedon in 1739, whilst another marriage at the same church was that of Ann Alvin, a widow of Hollym in 1742. Sadly, no link has ever been discovered between these people and the main character in our story.

Dramatis Personae

Details of the main characters in the story are now given in alphabetical order. The relevant sources, where applicable, are indicated by the following abbreviations:

A/C, D. S.	'The Accompt of David Sinclare, Administrator of the Goods, Rights, Creditts, Cattells and Chattells which lately were and did appertaine unto Enock Clerk late Vicar of Owthorne in the Dioces of York deceased.'B. I. A., ref CPH 4786 (undated)
Al. Cantab	J. & J. A. Venn, Alumni Cantabrigiensis, Vol IV, Part I to 1751, Cambridge University Press, 1927
B. I. A.	Borthwick Institute for Archives, York University
CDNB	Concise Dictionary of National Biography, Part I, Oxford University Press, 1961
E. R. Archives	County of East Riding of Yorkshire Archives, the Treasure House, Beverley
Cooper	T. P. Cooper, The History of the Castle of York, Elliot Stock, London, 1911
Gent	Thomas Gent, The History of the Royal and Beautiful Town of Kingston-upon-Hull, 1735
Hal. P. R.	The parish registers of All Saints, Halsham. E. R. Archives, PE15/2
Hed. P. R.	M. Craven, The Hedon Parish Registers, Vol I, Highgate Publications (Beverley) Ltd, 1993
Kil. P. R.	The parish registers of All Saints, Kilham. E. R. Archives, PE71/1-3
M. & R.	G. T. J. Miles and W. Richardson, A History of Withernsea, A. Brown & Sons, Hull, 1911
Miller	N. J. Miller, Winestead and its Lords, A. Brown & Sons, Hull, 1932
Owth. P. R.	The parish registers of St Peter's Owthorne. E. R. Archives, PE59/2
O. S.	Old style. Until the year 1752, England used the Julian calendar by which the new year always began on 25 March. Hence a date in a parish register of, say, February 1710, would equate to our 'modern' Gregorian reckoning of February 1711.
Park	G. R. Park The History of the Ancient Borough of Hedon, W. G. B. Page, Hull, 1895

Pat. P. R.   Rev H. E. Maddock (ed) The Registers of Patrington, The Yorkshire Parish Register Society, 1900

PMI   'A true and perfect Inventory of the goods, Cattles and Chattles moveable and Immoveable of Henock Sinclare Clerke late vicar of Owthorne alias Seathorne as they were Appraised by four men whose names are under written. B. I. A., ref CPH 4785 (undated)

Poulson   George Poulson, The History and Antiquities of the Seignory of Holderness, Robert Brown, Hull, 1840

St. Augustine's The parish church at Hedon

St. Peter's   The parish church at Owthorne

VCH   The Victoria History of the County of York East Riding; Oxford University Press
Vol II, J. D. Purdy, Kilham, 1974
Vol V, K. J. Allison and G. H. R. Kent, Holderness: Southern Part, 1984

Alvin, Adam:
Named as the murderer of the Rev Mr Henock Sinclare at an inquest held after the body was discovered. The verdict was reported in the burial entry of the vicar 25 April 1712. (Owth. P. R.)
Other documentary sources:

1   Owner of property at Owthorne with an annual value of £12, 1709-11. (Overseers' book, M. & R., p 253)

2   'Paid to Adam Alvin for wages due £6-0-0.' (A/C, D. S.)

3   Marriage entry, 29 August 1708. (Hal. P. R.)

4   'Item. Paid for other actions yet depending against this Accomptant (David Sinclare) at the Suit of Adam Alvin in the Court of Exchequer £10.' (A/C, D. S.)

5   Evidence of his execution appears in Dade's account, also Richard Fenby's memo and Gent, p 194.

Ashley, Bessy:
The owner of a lodging house near Hays Wharf, London. She and her nephew Will, a carrier by trade, are fictional characters.

Banks, Rev Robert:
Vicar of Holy Trinity church, Hull, 1689-1715.

Barritt, Laurence:
Members of the Barritt family appear in the Owth. P. R. from 1709 onwards. Laurence Barritt was buried in St Peter's churchyard 13 March 1737 (O. S.) The register describes him as 'an aged man'.

Bernardiston, Lady:
A property owner at Owthorne. 'Item, paid to the Lady Bernardiston for a quitt Rent, £3-8-0' (A/C, D.S.)
This lady was presumably the widow of Sir Samuel Bernardiston, 1620-1707, a prominent Whig politician and MP for Suffolk 1678-1707. (CDNB, p 63)

Bickerstaff, Ben:
The ostler at the Black Swan, Holborn. A fictional character.

Bradley, Tom:
The ostler at the King's Head inn, High Street, Hull. A fictional character.

Browne, Rev Jeremy:
Curate at Holy Trinity church Micklegate, York, who attended Alvin's execution. A fictional character.

Butler, Jed and Nan:
The proprietors of the Black Swan inn, Holborn. They are both fictional characters, but the inn did exist and a coach service, three days a week, between this inn and the Black Swan, Coney Street, York was established in 1706.

Blunt, Francis:
A minor Holderness gentry figure who died c 1710. He purchased the manor of Waxholme in 1650. (VCH Vol V, p 92) In 1687 he also owned Newton Garth in the parish of Paull. (VCH, Vol V, p 118)
'Item. Paid for Rent to Mr. Blunt due as aforesaid, £11.' (A/C, D. S.)

Chippendale, Edmund:
Chief gaoler a York Castle. Chippendale held this office from 1709 until 1718. (Cooper, p 310) 'Tom' his assistant is a fictional character.

Coleman, Robert:
Owner of a barn on Waxholme road rented by Henock Sinclare.
'Item. Paid to one Coleman for rent due as aforesaid, ten shillings.' (A/C, D. S.)
Robert first appears in the Owth. P. R. in 1692. In the following year he married Anne Batchelor at St Peter's. The couple probably removed from Owthorne before the time of the murder.

Cookman, Grimston:
The Cookmans were at Owthorne in the 1670s but there follows a gap of some sixty years before there are entries relating to the families of Joseph and Elizabeth Cookman and Francis and Ann Cookman. Joseph farmed at Rimswell and Francis was a freeholder of land in the Church Field of Withernsea.

Grimston was born to Francis and Ann and baptised at St Peter's on 11 May 1749. This was, of course, many years after the murder, but I liked the name and with author's licence I used it in the story.

Constable, Robert, 3rd Viscount Dunbar, 1651-1714:
Lord of the manor of Owthorne.

Dunns:
The family living at the Manor House, Patrington. George Dunn (d 1707) and his wife Ann (d 1701) had ten children, five of whom died in infancy. The eldest surviving child was Ann (1688-1731), who would have been twenty years old at the time of the murder. Her younger brother George, born 1694, would have been fourteen and the twins James and Frances, eight.

Fallowdown, Will:
The lad assisting John Jordan in the vicar's smallholding. His name usually appears in the Owth. P. R. as 'Falladown'. It looks as if he was actually employed by the vicar, as the A/C, D. S. lists a payment of 2s. 6d. 'to William Falladown for wages'. He married Frances Robson at St Peter's on 2 May 1707, and three of their children were baptised at the church. William was buried in the churchyard 19 April 1719. The register described him as 'a poor man'.

Fane, Sir Francis:
Lord of the manor of Kilham. He died in 1680. (VCH, Vol II, p 252)

Fiddes, Rev Dr Richard:
The rector of All Saints church, Halsham from 1696 until his death in 1725. He married Mary Sinclare and Adam Alvin at Halsham on 29 August 1708. (Hal. P. R., E. R. Archives, PE15/2)

Dr Fiddes was a notable theologian and an account of his work in that field is described in Poulson, Vol II, p 383.

The Christian names of his wife and son are fictional.

Galloway, Thomas:
A local shoemaker and beer-house keeper. This man first appears in the Owth. P. R. with the baptism of his daughter Margaret on 7 December 1680. His trade or profession is not recorded, but his burial entry of 4 February 1695 (O. S.) mentions that he was a resident of (South) Frodingham.

His part in this story is fictional.

Gibson, John:
A villager of Owthorne. There were a large number of Gibsons living at Owthorne and Rimswell dating from the mid-seventeenth century. At least three generations of sons were called John from 1681 onwards,

one being regularly referred to as a husbandman.

A John Gibson was buried at St Peter's on 20 March 1713 (O. S.) (Owth. P. R.)

Handson, Sarah:

A young servant girl at the vicarage. The Rev William Dade's account of the murder records there being a female domestic at the house, but does not mention her name. The real Sarah Handson, daughter of John and Sarah Handson, was baptised at St Peter's, 6 December 1697. This would make her about ten years old at the time of the murder.

Sarah's father John was described as a fisherman in the Owth. P. R.

Hutton, John:

The mate of the Billy Boy sailing from Hull. Both John and his son Tom are fictional characters.

Hutton, William:

A former manservant of Henock Sinclare. On 10 September 1707 he went to the East Riding Justices to lay unspecified charges against his master. Henock was obliged to appear at the following Quarter Sessions at Beverley. The outcome of the case is not known. Hutton was probably 'a bad lot'. (E. R. Archives, Quarter Sessions, QSF/4/C7)

Jeggar, John:

A villager at Owthorne. This man appears to have lived in the village all his life. Twice married, his union with Madaline Coates produced five children. He was married to a Jane Featherstone in 1700, producing two more children.

In 1681 Jeggar was the first witness to sign the memorandum of induction of Henock Sinclare as vicar of Owthorne. Jeggar was one of the two churchwardens at the time. (Owth. P. R.)

Joblin, Toby:

The ostler's boy at the Kings Head, High Street, Hull. A fictional character.

Jordan, John:

A man employed to look after the vicar's smallholding. In real life, Jordan married Elizabeth Wright at St Peter's in 1698 and two of their sons feature in the register of baptisms.

On 27 April 1710 Jordan, acting in the capacity of one of the churchwardens, 'signed' as one of the witnesses to a report made by the vicar of Rudstone and the rector of Roos, on the state of the vicarage and outbuildings. John signed by making his mark. He was described as a husbandman in his burial entry of 24 January 1720 (O. S.) (Owth. P. R.)

Kemp, Obediah:
A villager at Owthorne. In reality he was a husbandman of South Frodingham. His will is dated 25 November 1717 and he died about six months later. (B. I. A.)

Mason, Rev Charles:
Chaplain at York Castle gaol. The episode of this cleric dying in the middle of giving a sermon to the prisoners is fully described in Gent, p 194. It is also repeated in Dade's account of the murder, some fifty years later.

Owbridge, Samuel:
A tailor at Owthorne. The petition by this man to the E R Justices for expenses incurred whilst staying at York to give evidence against Adam and Mary Alvin is crucial to the telling of the story. (E. R. Archives, Quarter Sessions, QSP99)
Owbridge died at Owthorne and was buried there on 19 September 1725. (Owth. P. R.)

Pighills, Rev John:
The rector of St Patrick's church at Patrington. The Al. Cantab. states that he was a sizar at Christ's College and matriculated in July 1676. He was the rector of Patrington from 1685 until his death in August 1725. He is buried at Patrington.

Pighills, Phyllis:
Wife of the rector of Patrington. This lady's real Christian name may have been Elizabeth. In Henock Sinclare's PMI, under 'Disperate Debts' owing to the vicar, is the entry, 'Oweing by Elizabeth Piggells, £10. 0. 0.' I can find no entry for the burial of this lady in the Pat. P. R.

Preston, Widow:
A shopkeeper at Owthorne. Mary Preston was probably the widow of Matthew Preston. They married at Owthorne in 1677. Matthew became a churchwarden and signed as one of the witnesses to the 1681 memorandum of the induction of Henock Sinclare.
Mary Preston was buried at St Peter's on 7 November 1720. (Owth. P. R.)

Prowde, Rev Samuel:
Curate at St Augustine's. Park states, 'In 1698 the name "Sam Prowde, Cur de Hedon' appears in the register.'

This cleric was probably the son of the Rev Samuel Prowde, rector of St Patrick's, Patrington from 1661 to 1682. The Pat. P. R. has the entry of the baptism of Samuel Jnr on 19 March 1662 (O. S.)

Sinclare, Catherine:
The younger niece of Henock Sinclare, living at the vicarage and an accomplice to the crime. Neither Dade nor Richard Fenby identify her, but the forename, 'Catherine' is first given in the account by M. & R. in 1911. All sources, however, agree that she had some serious illness and to ease her conscience she revealed the whereabouts of her uncle's body by some unspoken sign.

There is no proof that Catherine ever went to live with the Dunns at Patrington, and she does not appear in the list of burials of the Pat. P. R.

Sinclare, David:
The half-brother of Henock and a freehold farmer at Kilham on the Yorkshire Wolds. Born 1654, he was the eldest son of David Sinclare (died 1660) of Kilham by his first wife.

David became the administrator of the goods and chattels of his half-brother. His surviving A/C, D. S. casts a strong light on the story post the murder. The document is undated but refers to the PMI. It reveals that several searches were made to find the missing vicar who, 'as yet has not been found or heard of . . . '

The account mentions the robbery at the vicarage, the recovery of the stolen goods and 'the taking of the thief to York gaol'. Also listed is the payment to Adam Alvin of £6 'for wages due'.

David Sinclare was obviously quite a litigious character, and one who experienced great inconvenience in the collection of debts owing to Henock.

Sinclare, Rev Henock:
Vicar of St Leonard's New Malton and the uncle of the murder victim.

Born at Kilham of farming stock, he was at Malton by 1666, as the parish register there records the burial of his wife, Anne, on 4 April.

Henock's will, written in 1671, makes a number of bequests, one of which was the gift of his books to his nephew Henock. (B. I. A.)

Henock Snr was buried at St Leonard's 15 November 1678.

Sinclare, Rev Henock:
The vicar of Owthorne 1681-1708. Born 10 March 1656 (O. S.) to David Sinclare and his second wife Lucy, at Kilham. (E. R. Archives, PE71/1)

Murdered by his manservant Adam Alvin, 10 June 1708, his body was not found until 18 April 1712. (Owth. P. R.)

Sinclare, Lucy:

Mother of George, Henock and Samuel, who were named as joint executors of her will, written on 1 January 1670. (O. S.)

At the time of making her will, she was a relatively well-off widow and was able to leave four oxgangs of arable land in the Northside fields of Kilham to her eldest son, George. (B. I. A.)

Sinclare, Mary:

The elder niece of Henock, living at the vicarage and the main party to the crime.

I have been unable to trace the birth or the parentage of Mary. Two sources confirm her forename. The first is the entry of her marriage to Adam in the Hal. P. R., and the second, the petition of Samuel Owbridge to the E. R. Justices.

What became of Mary after she was acquitted at the York assizes is not known.

Sinclare, Samuel:

The younger brother of the murder victim, born c 1659 to David and Lucy Sinclare. He appears as a joint executor with his brothers in the will of his mother 1670.

The story of him being the father of Mary and Catherine is fictional, as also is his supposed disappearance to the Americas to seek his fortune. The baptismal register of St Peter's does have one obviously related entry: 'April 29th. 1695, Lucy, daughter of Samuel Sinclare.' Why Lucy was baptised at Owthorne is not known, but this woman may have played another part in the story. In the petition of Samuel Owbridge to the E R Justices for claiming expenses relating to his journey to the trial at York, it was directed that he 'did bring the body of Lucy Sinclare Spinster another Evidence agt the said Prisoners from the Castle of York to Kingston upon Hull and paid the Charges during the Journey'. (E. R. Archives, Quarter Sessions QSP99)

Sissison, Rev Richard:

The vicar of Hedon 1697-1730 and vicar of Owthorne 1708-30. He was probably also the rector of Preston, although his name does not appear in Poulson's list of rectors. (Vol II, p 185)

The son of a shoemaker, Sissison was born and educated at Beverley. Admitted a sizar at St John's College, Cambridge at the age of seventeen, he obtained his degree in 1690 and was ordained a deacon at York in the same year. (Al. Cantab.)

He died in 1730 and was buried in St Augustine's.

Tolly, Henry:
The master of the Billy Boy sailing from Hull. A fictional character.

Turner, John:
Manservant to the rector of Patrington. A fictional character.

Tymm, Leonard:
An apothecary, resident at Hedon. This man's origins are not known, but *The East Riding Medical Men*, J A R & M E Bickford, Yorkshire Family History Society, 2007, may be in error in quoting him as, 'of Howden'.

He had two daughters baptised at St Augustine's: Christiana 1732 and Ann 1736. He was buried in St Augustine's 21 July 1738. (Hed. P. R. Vol I, p 162)

Waterland, Henry:
An attorney-at-law residing at the Old Hall, Hedon. Waterland was baptised at Flixborough, North Lincs on 11 September 1673. He came to Hedon about the year 1696 and set up a lawyer's practice there. His wall monument in St Augustine's records that 'he practised the arduous profession of the law with great integrity for seventy years'.

In the year 1700 he married Martha Baines, the daughter of Alderman William Baines, and in time served the borough as mayor on eight occasions.

Waterland's half-brother, the Reverend Daniel Waterland, DD, became Chancellor of York Minster and a prebend of Windsor.

For a full description of Henry and his family, see *The Waterland Story*, V A Reeves and M Craven, 2007.

Wright, Samuel:
Clerk to Henry Waterland at Hedon. Wright's birthplace is unknown, but he was resident at Hedon by 1701, when he signed as a witness to an indenture of release of property in St Augustine's gate. (Author's collection)

The Hed. P. R. show that he was a qualified attorney by 1718 and is accorded the title of 'Mr' in several baptismal entries of his children. He was buried at St Augustine's on 23 April 1763. (Hed P. R., Vol I, p 166)

Acknowledgements

First and foremost I should like to thank two ladies whose guidance and continued support to me throughout the writing of this book has been invaluable. To Pauline Ashurst go my sincere thanks for reading and re-reading the drafts, correcting my mistakes, reducing 'the history', and making many suggestions to improve the text. In a similar vein, I am indebted to Valerie Wood, who took much trouble and time from her busy writing schedule to suggest ways to convert my dull prose into a readable novel form. Any success which might come to this work is largely due to their guidance and help.

Concerning specific areas, I wish to thank the following people for their help and information: Dr David Neave for locating many of the documentary sources at York and Beverley; Gerald Procter, MBE, for legal matters in the eighteenth century; Arthur Credland for suggesting the 'Billy Boy' and advising on other relevant maritime details; the late Dr J A R Bickford for medical procedures; Peter Jenkinson for suggesting Hays Wharf and for sharing with me his intimate knowledge of the City of London; Professor Bernard Jennings for Kilham details.

Also for kind assistance given: Ian Mason, Archives and Local Studies Manager at the Treasure House, Beverley; Mrs Rita Freedman, City Archivist at the York City Archives; the late Fr Michael O'Connor; Tony Craven; John Ruston, MBE; Chris Webb at the Borthwick Institute for Archives, York; the Rev J A Wardle, Rural Dean of Bridlington; the Rev Ronald Howard, Rural Dean for South Holderness Deanery; Dr David Connell, Director of Burton Constable Foundation, and Tina Hamson for searching through the records of assizes at Kew.

Finally, I should like to thank Sue Hyde for her great skill and patience in converting my rough longhand pages into printable type and for editing the final version.

Martin Craven
Hessle, May 2009

Mr Henock Sinclare was Vicar of Swtham 50 Years
John Westerdale & Rich. Fenby knew the woman who so
him Taken up out of the place where he was Concealed
and she said his Brains appeared when taken up and
she said that she never Could Eate any Brains of any
kind after; her Name was Ann Gargill she died in the
100 Year of her Age; the report was he was Murdered with
Spade and his Skull was laid Open; and the man Adam
Alvin took his Horse and Hat & Whip as far as Whitin
Stolen near a well to prevent any Suspicion; his Coffin
sliped down Cliff from the South Isle of The Curch about
18 Years ago; and it was reinterred in the Low part of Church
Yard being a lead one and is near Cliff again ——
There was two Nieces lived with him at the time he was
Murdered and Adam Alvin wanted to Marrey one of them
and they got Married after and went to Lincolnshire and kept
a publick House at the time he was taken the report was
the other Could not rest well untill she made a discovery
by droping a glove on the place where he was Concealed
the woman was tried by a Conoror inquest and Hanged

Withernsea July 1 1827

I remain Your Most Obt.

Rich Fenby

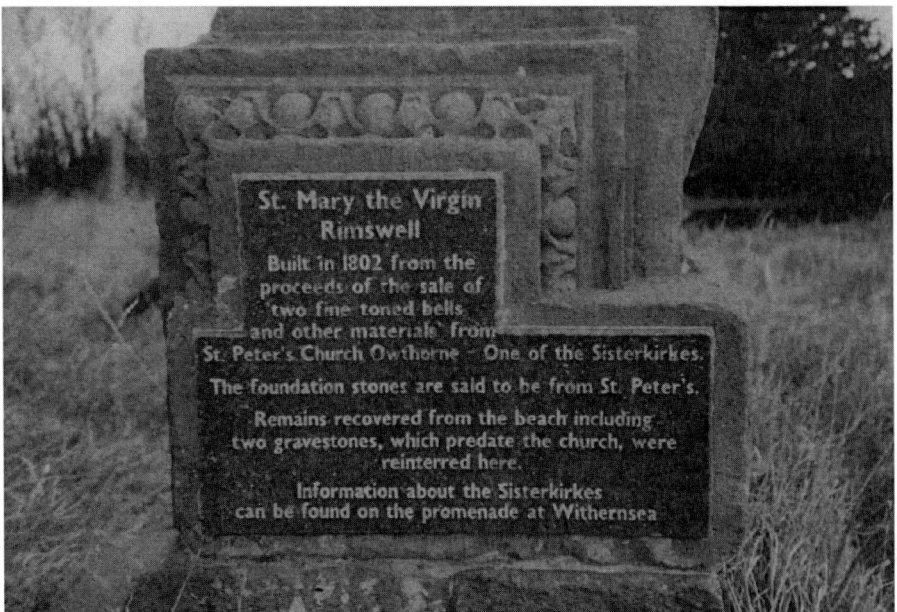

The last vestiges of St. Peter's church at Owthorne as recorded on a plaque in the churchyard at Rimswell. Photograph by the author 2006.

Memorandum of the induction of Henock Sinclare as vicar of Owthorne in 1681.
A page from the parish register of St. Peter's, Owthorne, reproduced by kind permission of the Rev^d. Mr. Ronald Howard, Rural Dean for the South Holderness Deamery.

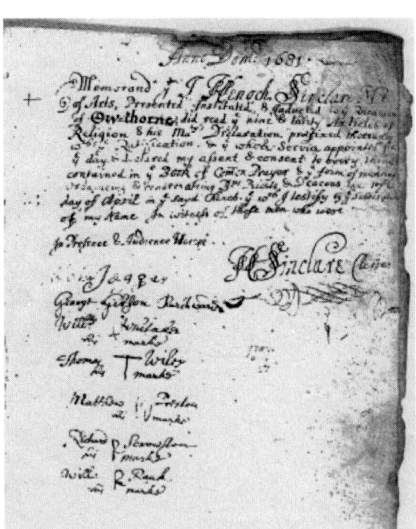

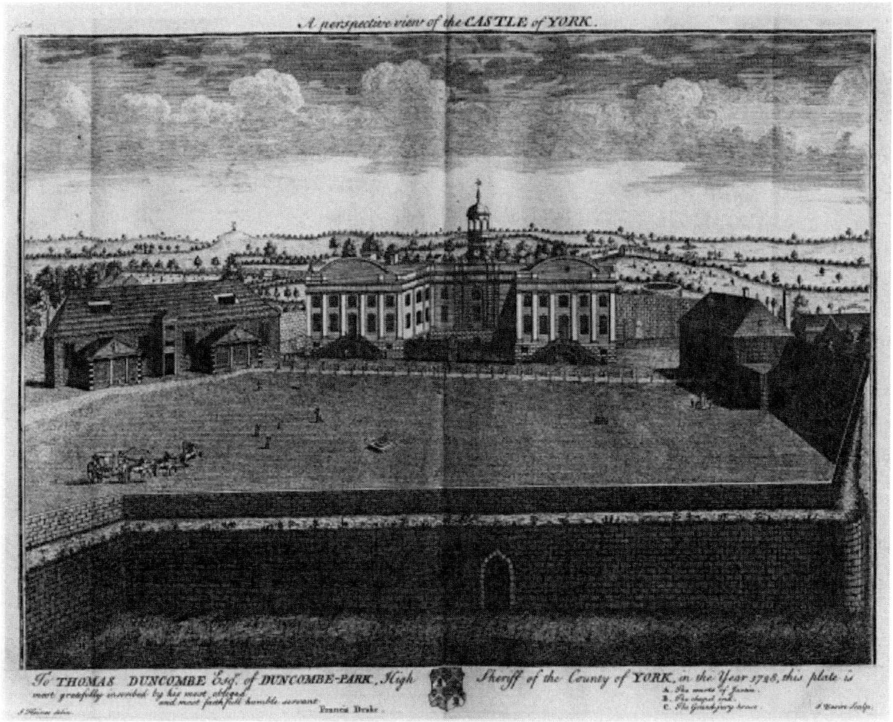

A perspective view of the CASTLE of YORK.

To THOMAS DUNCOMBE Esq. of DUNCOMBE-PARK, High Sheriff of the County of YORK, in the Year 1728, this plate is most gratefully inscribed by his most obliged and most faithful humble servant Francis Drake

The new gaol and court complex at York Castle where Adam and Mary Alvin were incarserated and tried.
A view taken from Drake's *History Of York* 1728.

The condemned cell in York Castle gaol where Adam Alvin would have spent his last hours.
An image reproduced by kind permission of York City Archives.

157

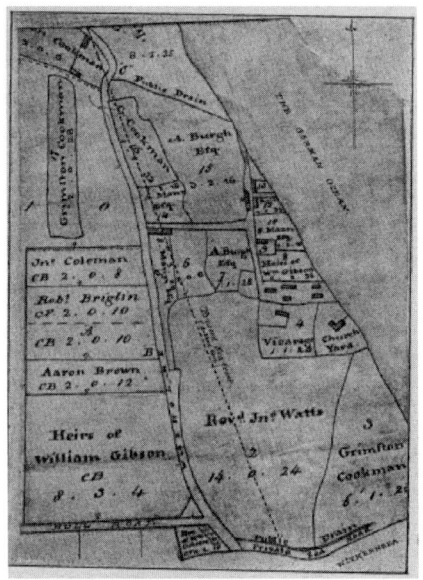

A section of the Enclosure map of Owthorne, showing the Vicarage and the Church yard, by Robert Stickney, 1806.
Reproduced from Miles & Richardson's *History of Withernsea*, 1911.

A model of a Billy Boy sailing ship on display in the Maritime Museum at Hull.
Photograph by the author with kind permission of Hull City Museums.

A Murder.

The year 1708 is distinguished in the little annals of this parish, by the Murder of the Vicar. Mr. Sinclair had been instituted to the living fourteen years; his Family, besides himself, consisted of two Nieces, & two Domestics, a Male & Female. The Man Servant who will be long remembered under the name of Alvin, was now about 25 Years of Age, & having captivated the affections of the elder Niece they entertained a reciprocal passion. Whether from the Idea of removing the obstacle to his mutual wishes, or of enlarging at once his fortune & his happiness, so it was, Alvin, sought the destruction of his Master. He ventured to disclose the black design to the two Sisters, who scrupled not to be Accomplices in his Guilt. The plot conducted with great secrecy, was carried

attempted, by leaving the Country, to fly from Justice, & sought to dissipate the terrors of their guilty minds in a crouded Metropolis. But vain were their attempts; for avenging Heaven, tho' slowly, yet with unerring steps, pursued them. For nearly four years, they escaped the punishment due to so great an enormity; at the close of which period, the Younger Sister in which she was stung with remorse arrested by a sudden & fatal sickness, exhibited dreadful perturbations of Mind, and unable to articulate, she intimated by signs where the Body of her Uncle might be found. Search was accordingly made, and on the 18 April 1712, the remains of Mr. Sinclair were discovered at the bottom of a ditch within the Yard, five yards from adjoining the house, covered with

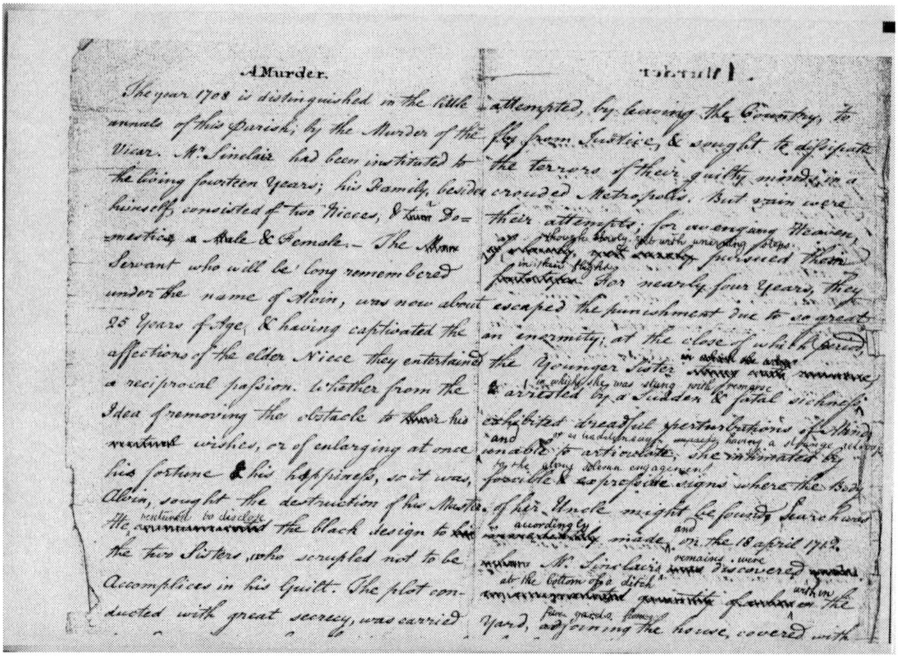

Extracts from the account of the murder written by the Reverend William Dade, c. 1785.
Amendments to the text probably made by George Poulson.
Reproduced by kind permission of the Burton Constable Foundation and Dr. David Connell.

1712

Mr Henock Sinclare Vicar of Owthorne Buried in ye South Isle joining on ye Chancel — April ye 25th —
He was murdered by his Man Servt Adam Alvin June ye 10th 1708 & laid concealed in ye Ground in a Pit abt five yards from ye Vicarage House, till the 10th of April 1712. — & upon ye 20th of ye same Month, was found upon an Inquest of ye Crowner & Jury, to be so murdered by ye Man aforesaid
Thomas Son of Jno Brunfil Buried — — May ye 30th 1712.
Margaret ye Wife of John Gibson Senr Buried January ye 23d —
William Son of John Brunsil Buried — Febry ye 13th
Ann Gentleman of Frodingham buried — March ye 21st

1713

John Gibson was Buried — March ye 20th 1713.

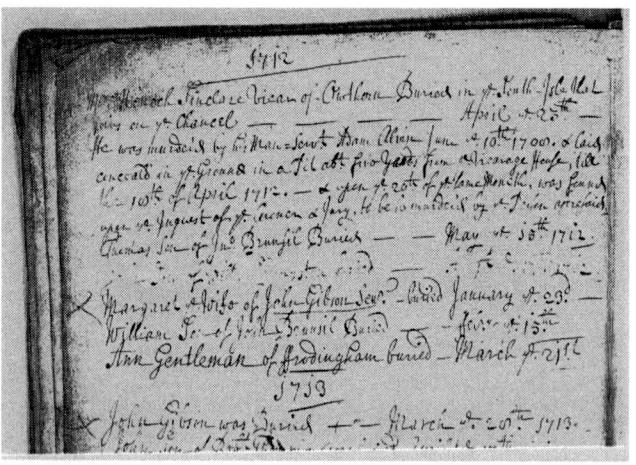

An extract from the parish register of St. Peter's, Owthorne, recording the burial of Henock Sinclare, 25 April 1712 and the result of the inquest held five days earlier. Reproduced with kind permission of the Revd. Mr. R. Howard, Rural Dean South Holderness.

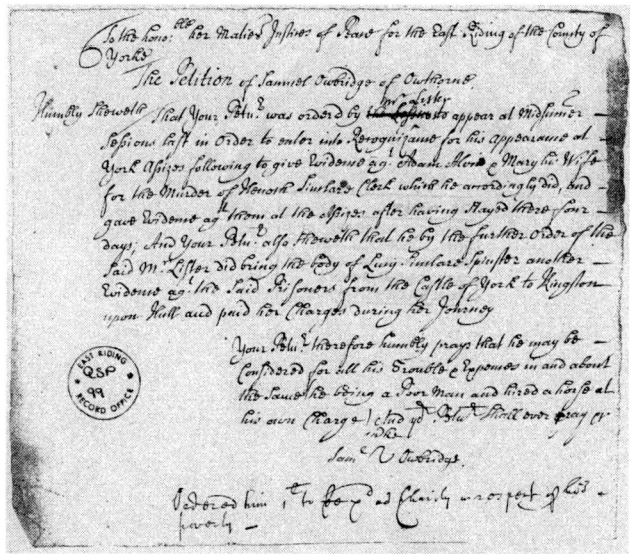

YORK Four Days Stage-Coach.

Begins on Friday the 12th. of April 1706.

ALL that are desirous to pass from *London* to *York*, or from *York* to *London*, or any other Place on-that Road; Let them Repair to the *Black Swan* in *Holbourn* in *London*, and to the *Black Swan* in *Coney* *street* in *York*.

At both which Places, they may be received in a Stage Coach every *Monday*, *Wednesday* and *Friday*, which performs the whole Journey in Four Days. (*if God permits*.) And sets forth at Five in the Morning.

And returns from *York* to *Stamford* in two days, and from *Stamford* by *Huntington* to *London* in two days more. And the like Stages on their return.

Allowing each Passenger 14l. weight, and all above 3d. a Pound.

Performed By { *Benjamin Kingman*, *Henry Harrison*, *Walter Baynes*,

Also this gives Notice that *Newcastle* Stage Coach, sets out from *York*, every Monday, and Friday, and from *Newcastle* every Monday, and Friday.

A stage-coach bill from the Black Swan Inn, Coney Street, York announcing a 4-day service to London.

The petition made by Samuel Owbridge, a tailor from Owthorne, to the East Riding Justices, claiming expenses for travelling between Holderness and York to give evidence at the trail of Adam and Mary Alvin.

The JPs have written at the foot of the petition: 'Ordered him £1 to be P.d as Charity in respect of his poverty.'

Reproduced by kind permission of Mr. Ian Mason, Archives and Local Studies Manager, the Treasure House, Beverley.